T0062891

CIRCUMSTANCES
GREW HIM UP

CIRCUMSTANCES
GREW HIM UP

COLORS OF LIFE

Satish B3 Anand

PARTRIDGE

To order additional copies of this book, contact
Partridge India
000 800 10062 62
orders.india@partridgepublishing.com

www.partridgepublishing.com/india

Preface –
CIRCUMSTANCES GREW HIM UP

In this work an attempt has been made, by assembling the struggles made by Pushpraj for his family and love life, to give the reader an idea of the part which he overcomes by facing unfavorable circumstances strongly that comes in his way. Pushpraj a boy born in a family whose father works as a sweeper, brought up amongst several discriminations only because he comes from a family which does not have the status that of others.

Pushpraj participates in singing competition and his name is not called only because he is son of a sweeper. He gets determined and bags winning medal and trophy for the school. And this son of a sweeper gives his school a recognition as that's the first medal and trophy his school has ever received before. This way he becomes a singer and bags 02 medals and 18 awards just in 09 years. He never gives up.

Pushpraj wants to be a doctor after 10+2 but could not become due to financial crisis in his family. He firms up decision of escaping from home and take up a job to provide financial support to family so that his younger one's do not suffer and remain away from their dream that they desire. He runs away from home and remains missing. Nobody knows about pushpraj; where is he? In which condition he is? It's been 02 months and family is mourning. But he calls a day, when receives his salary and sends money order for his family.

Love attacks Pushpraj. He falls in love with a girl but never expresses his feelings. Neither Pushpraj nor the girl. They both know; they love each other but fear of losing overpowers their true feelings. Pushpraj gets enganged to some other girl. Post engagement pushpraj and the girl whom he falls in love come to know about their love. They propose each other and decide to marry. Pushpraj decides to break the engagement as in to marry his love. He breaks the engagement. He is dragged to court. He is processed under legal actions but he keeps his love away from all problems. Pushpraj's love backs off and then he gets paralysis hit and loses his job, image and his love as well. His left remains paralyzed till death. He rises back again.

After 6.5 years he again falls in love with Gurpreet. He does not have any faith in love scenarios that is why he didn't allow any girl to enter in his life. But gurpreet is different, He falls in love and she too partially means her conducts displays love for Pushpraj. She asks pushpraj to sing and write for her till death. He writes everyday for her and he wishes to have her as she is her only desire. He loves him and he will achieve her any how.

Pushpraj is a super hero. He is a Winner over unfavorable circumstances. Pushpraj's story gives all us a message;

"Learn from Circumstances"

Every minute, every moment, and at every step, We come across circumstances. Circumstances which are unavoidable and unfavorable. What should we do? Shall we negate or we fight? Or else, we go neutral leaving the result on to the destiny? We have to be truly different as we should fight and face. We should consider it as an opportunity because we know the fact that these unfavorable circumstances are temporary and these are here to teach us lessons for a better life. We will have to fight as this life is not ours, It belongs to our Progenitors and those who love and care for us like anything. Hence, we need to give a POSITIVE display and projection of ourselves so that we set an example for others to follow.

We can't leave it on destiny, we need to act as Almighty says, "He helps them those who help themselves" and We must and definitely help ourselves. We have got no option, It's our life. So, We need to fight against it to taste SUCCESS and to absorb the RAYS of HAPPINESS to prove as a WINNER.

Don't negate, Face and act to the circumstances that come across. Display the WINNING attitude and be a REAL HERO......

Warm Wishes,
Satish Anand

GRATITUDE TO FAIR LOVERS

Mummy and Papa your trusts are the most important to me. Mummy and Papa the trusts of you are the supporter to me to do the best in my life. Mummy and Papa, please stay at my sides until the end. The only god I have seen on this earth is you both. You are my world.

Thank you Mummy, without your support authoring book was not possible. I know how did you manage money and gave me to publish. I shall never forget your unconditional love. I feel lucky that I HAVE YOU....

Thank you Papa. You are "Man of Struggles". A man who stands tall in front of all the struggles. You made me to understand the true meaning of life & humanity.

Thank you dear Elder Brother Amit, you are copy of Mr. Father. Your simplicity and your humbleness are your jewels. Thank you dear Ravi (Younger Brother). Being young, you teach lessons of unity to us and try to bring us closer whenever we fight and stay disconnected.

Thank you dear Sarita (Youngest amongst all siblings). You are the 02nd beautiful woman after our mother we have ever seen in our lives. At the age of 10 you started taking care for the entire family when mother went unwell and couldn't take up responsibilities after that due to her sickness. You still know our likes and dislikes. you know our everything. We love you all. Thank you Dear Balwant Babu (Sarita's Husband & Neuro Surgeon). We are lucky to have you in our life and we feel privileged for our sister that she has a loving and caring husband. You are so simple and down to earth we have ever seen. You are the one who defines kindness. Thank you to our neice Simran Kaur (Sarita's daughter). She is our lifeline especially for my mother. She calls mother as Maiya, Elder Brother as Balle, Chotu bhai to me and Bibbi to Ravi. She is the cutest kid of this world.

HEARTIEST THANKS TO B3

Dear B3, Without you, I do not know where I would be. You have made a major difference in my life. I gave you hard times but you put up with me. Just want to say never mind my words.

Things were not just the same without you. It's great to have you in life.

Can't afford to lose you........

FOR A MENTOR, FROM WHOM I HAVE LEARNT THE VITAL SKILL OF LIFE & WHO MADE ME WHO I AM

I would like to express my deepest thanks to **Vishal Kehr Sir**. His patience, encouragement and immense knowledge were key motivations throughout. He carries out his work with an objective and principled approach towards everything and that is the thing which makes him my MENTOR and of course the only FAIR MENTOR I have ever seen in my life.

FOR A TRUE FRIEND

I WOULD LIKE TO EXTEND SINCERE THANKS TO **Piyush Singhal Ji**. You should know your support and encouragement was worth more than I can express on paper. Thank you for your enthusiasm, pride and curiosity. Will never forget the time spent together, those days were the best days of my life.

TO THE FOUR SUPPORTING HANDS WHO SHARED THEIR WORK FOR THE BOOK

My deep appreciation and a huge thank you to fair supporters who play a significant role in making this effort possible.

Ram Pal Singh Rathore Sir who has shooted Video for the book to gain maximum reach- thank you Sir for your patience and persistence. I am truly obliged on the act of kindness. I am sure the video would help me a lot to make my book reach to max...

This book was incomplete without the sketches. So, I want to extend thanks to **Sonal Vidyarthi** for the beautiful sketches given for the book and to tolerate me for asking to make changes in the sketches again and again. But you should know you are superb...

I am also thankful to **Ankita Verma** who helped me with amazing sketches. I remember it was late night when she came to give me the sketches. I really appreciate the sincerity shown. She has been great...

I would like to acknowledge and express sincere thanks to Artist and a friend **Smriti Jadon** for use of her art work for the book COVER PAGE. Thank you so much for presenting the beautiful artwork. I am very pleased to have such enormous and magnificent work from you. Thank you for not losing hope. You are simply awesome....

1

HE IS A SWEEPER'S SON"

He was a 'Band Wala', 'Bhangre Wala', A sweeper's son. These were the identities that he had. A boy belonged to a family whose father was a SWEEPER & owned a Band shop in Mayapur.

Have you ever played Casio S-21 and sung on Band trolley in client's wedding procession? Have you ever sung "Aaj Mere Yaar Ki Shaadi Hai", "Yeh Desh Hai Veero Jawano Ka" the most favorite and preferred tracks, not just preferred in fact the starting tracks for all the wedding processions?

Have you ever played "Dhoom Dhoom Lak Lak" the freaking Punjabi rhythm having dressed up like Bhangre Wala in the mid of indistinct crowds and several occasions?

Having Turla (fan like adornment on the Turban), Pag (turban–the pride of Bhangra dress), Kaintha (Necklace), Kurta (similar to silk short), Lungi (A loose loincloth tied around the drummer's waist) & Jugi (A waist coat) & having Punjabi DHOL (cylindrical shaped drum) slung round the neck with two sticks in the hand and producing Bhangra Rhythm and making people mince, dance and shake their body, lifting hands up in the air and trying to perform partial Bhangra–which almost everybody does in joyful situations.

PUSHPRAJ has done this all and still he did whenever required. So introducing the BAND WALA, BHANGRE WALA, A SWEEPER'S son in front of you all. Meet the man "PUSHPRAJ".

Change is the only constant thing in this world. He too changed, his personality changed as he grew up and he grew up as per the circumstances that came across his way in life. He had many dreams and desire but all those were wiped & snatched away from him by those unfavorable circumstances. He could never become, what he wished. He became what his circumstances had for him. Whatever he was he was because of the circumstances and always felt lucky about him and expressed gratitude to the circumstances that came across his way. He relied on 3 friends only, the friends who are genuine and true.... Their names are-PASSION, DETERMINATION & DEDICATION.....

2

PUSHPRAJ-A BAND WALA

He was a simple and humble person in behavior. He was a human who always remained down to earth enjoying life..... Whatever had god blessed him with? Enjoying life for him was just normal. He was genuinely down to earth. Its human nature and tendency to change attitude, behavior, conduct which is arrogant for others. People forget their past, their living in past, the circumstances and change their behavior as well.

Pushpraj remained same as he was before. He had sung on band trolley, played Punjabi drum (Bhangra) whenever required. I mean whenever workers were short in his own Band Baja. However, he loved performing songs and playing drum in bookings. Frankly telling even after achieving great recognition and being on a good position he continued performing in his Brass band. He had a huge fan following. There were thousands who admired him, followed him and many wished to be like him. He was quite popular and famous. Even then he did not bother about his image and status only because that was the place where he came and so why be shy and why be hesitant. So he loved performing songs on band trolley and playing Drum (Punjabi).

The best thing was that he always found people in wedding procession, Religious procession who were standing next to the trolley and listening his songs curiously and that made him happy.

In Band parties; abuses, hatred, discrimination feeling of rich and poor is very obvious, hence he was always prepared as he knew that he will find many who would abuse him and say hell lot of shit but he has to ignore all by saying SORRY again and again and all over again with smile.

It's unbelievable that he was putting up Punjabi drum and played in engagement, wedding ceremonies having slung over the neck. The good thing was that he was a good Drummer. The instance he would start the striking beat switching over to "Dhoom Lak Lak", people would move their feet, mince and dance. He knew several beats like Bhangra, Dandiya, folk, Twist etc. having Dagga in left and Thili (stick) in right hand.

Can you imagine playing Dhol (Drum) slung over the neck being mobile in wedding procession. You play in full swing and then somebody comes and pulls your waist coat, abuses and says "play here the fast beat and don't move, play as fast as you can". And you listen their orders, abuses and then you give your hands a momentum to play faster and harder, lest you will be slapped or abused any time. Can you ever imagine, people holding edge of currency note in their mouth and they want you to get that note in your mouth by approaching the person's mouth and holding the other end of the currency note. And you play the beat faster and harder holding note in mouth and ensuring the pace doesn't slow down. Can you ever imagine people holding currency note in their hands up in the air and they want you to catch the note. But when you try to get the note they go taller by raising their hands high. And finally you get. But sometimes people just pretend to offer the note but they don't want you to come and catch. If you ever try to catch, you are abused..... This all had happened with Pushpraj.

The question is will people start devaluing him? Will his identity fade away? Will people be at a distance now? May be? Now the world would know his background that he was "SON OF A SWEEPER", he was a "BAND WALA", "A BHANGRA WALA". But this was a fact! That he was, and he will always be. Can he change his fate? Can he change his past? No one in this world can do that so he always took pride in saying "He was "SON OF A SWEEPER". And let him be that.....

Pushpraj looked smart in that dress, I mean Bhangra dress. He also played Jhunjhuna wearing Band uniform from top to bottom dressed in Red color coat, Black pant, cap on head, Thick Red belt on waist, Anklet on lower part of legs. He never felt shy, ashamed of work.

So yes Pushpraj was a BAND WALA.....

3

THE SIXTH DAY STORY

Pushpraj's father was a Man of struggles. He was above 80. He and the whole family strongly believed that Mr. Father was one piece in this world. Nobody was like him. He had faced struggles throughout his life like anything "but what's new about it? As almost everybody would have faced struggles as struggles are part of one's life. This question would arise in the Reader's heart & soul too..... The thing and the attribute which made him different was never complaining attitude. Mr. Father had never shared about his struggles that came his way. Pushpraj and the family came to know about it from mother and that too whenever they were armed by the boundaries of sorrows. Sorrows which were the results of

Mr. Father's kindness & love for their own dear ones who hurt and they were none other than his own step Mother, step Brothers and the people who flourished under the holy shower of love & happiness of Mr. Father.

Betrayal has become human tendency and that's why Establishing faith and Trust has become difficult and so humanity is vanishing. LOVE, TRUST & RESPECT are the three pillars required for following the holiest religion "Humanity". Human values and ethics have taken down fall as these three pillars don't exist in humanity. That's why, very few come up to help those who look forward for it. There is a saying "Do good and cast in to the river". Pushpraj and his father both strongly followed the policy. Imagine, what would happen if all of us withdraw our hands back and get determined not to help anybody. That would be "End to Humanity". This is what Mr. Father didn't do. He continued helping, supporting, loving caring people ignoring ill results which would come across later when he himself would be looking for the support.

I wrote about Pushpraj's father as pushpraj had learnt all from his father and that's why he always took pride in saying "He was SON OF A SWEEPER".

It was raining like cats and dogs and it rained continuously for more than 7 hours. Pushpraj was 05 years old and it was his 6th day to school as he had just started going to school. He was in LKG. He was sent to the best school of the town though he belonged to middle class. As said it was raining heavily. The school got off. Pushpraj reserved his corner seat in school Rickshaw and suited himself for way back home. The school was not that far, it was just at a distance of 1.5 kilometers. Rickshaw driver dropped him to the lane, a narrow lane connecting his house. Pushpraj got wet in just 40-50 seconds. He got inside the house calling his mother shouting loudly with joy as stories were ready to be shared to the mother. Normally, His mother would change dress and Pushpraj would recite all the stories, funny stories created by himself which would bring smile on his mother's face and would cherish. But this 6th day stories were untold to his mother as he found his uncles and aunties & their kids & Grandmother sitting in his parent's room. This little kid didn't know that his parent's room was no more of his parents. He was unaware, that was no more his house. He didn't know that his parents and his 8 years old elder brother were forcefully thrown out of the house. He didn't know that his mother was thrashed by foots by uncle and was asked to move out.

Pushpraj sensed anger, hatred from all those who were sitting in the room. He asked to his Aunty-Chachi (Aunty) where Mummy is. His question was not answered. Rather pushpraj was said Manhoos (Gloomy). chotu, raja beta, Beta, bachcha were the names his Mom and Dad used to take to call him. He was small but he could understand the words expressing love and the words displaying hatred and anger. "Manhoos" was a new word for him as he was never called by such words before. He understood these people don't love him at all and then the Elder brother came in few minutes and took him away from there to "Madai" (A small hut on the main road).

His mother was groaning, whining from pain as she was thrashed by them. She was shouting and they could do nothing as they were helpless.

There were buckets, boilers placed under to avoid water falling on the floor. The roof was leaking at many places. Pushpraj was hungry and he expressed his hungriness to his mother. And mother was helpless as that MADAI had no cooking arrangement. Neither had bed to sleep nor food to eat. Mr. Father couldn't see them tormenting from Hunger. He went outside without bothering Rain to a shop to organize food for all. He got Namkeen (Crunchy Savoury Snack) and Samosa (Pie) for them which were wrapped in a piece of Hindi Newspaper. They all had together though it was tasteless as they all got wet in rain but it sufficed their hunger for a time being.

Mr. Father was strictly asked to move empty handed to MADAI except having the Khatiya (COT). He got the COT as it was the bed which was gifted to him in his wedding. Mr. Father knew running family now would be difficult task and will not be able to organize daily bread. So he decided to send his family and Pushpraj to his matrimonial home Sahabganj till the things come back to normal. Patience, Contentment, Gratification are the jewels of Mr. Father's personality as it leaded to huge Bungalow on the road side replacing MADAI (HUT) beautifully constructed. However, it took him years to construct huge Bungalow. And the house from where he was evacuated is now just RUINS. He never complained, neither he fought nor he raised his voice for the property that fell in his part. He left everything and never complained as he loved his both brothers and Mother and their kids knowing that they are steps. "He loved them as he never listened any ill words for his brothers whenever somebody spoke.

Do good and cast into the RIVER....Mr. Father followed and so did the Pushpraj....

Mr. Father always said; nothing can stop him from loving his brothers. His honesty, compassion and forgiveness made him everyone's Ideal person.

That's why he was pushpraj's ideal person. He was the one whom pushpraj admired. He was the only one whom he loved to follow and did all what his father did for others and let Humanity exist & let love, Trust & Respect Breed and flourish in one's heart & soul.

This way, sixth day story remained untold.....

4

LOVE SCENE in 7TH CLASS.

Manpreet spoiled his fair (Pushpraj) notebook by drawing hearts, infinite hearts separated by an arrow and writing the 1st letter of Pushpraj i.e. P and hers i.e. M.

Pushpraj was in 7th standard. He studied in HOLY CROSS School at Mayapur and that was the best school of the town. He was just 13 or 14. He was not that studious though he was trying his best to perform and deliver but couldn't come amongst Rankers and performers. He had interest in extra-curricular activities and he was good at it. Pushpraj used to be calm and quite in school. He was never that active. He was serious, sincere towards his studies, that's why he was loved by all the teachers. There had been a Moral science teacher Ms. Magleen and

Pushpraj was very amicable to her. She was like Mother to him. He sensed motherly love whenever he was with her. Her lessons taught were life lessons which taught him to be kind to everyone introducing yourself as you will never regret being kind". She said our religion should be kindness. It's very obvious today we see humans but no humanity only because kindness is vanished from our hearts and souls. Pushpraj implemented her lessons in his life which brought him success and made him a true human.

Pushpraj started his love career in VIIth standard but couldn't succeed. A Biology teacher who was class teacher as well wanted silence in his class and if anybody made noise was asked to move out of the class. Manpreet was notorious, very naughty and created disturbance a lot in the class. In fact, she was the most mischievous girl of the class.

Once a day she was caught murmuring song inside the class which broke teacher's lecture's flow. Class Teacher was a good teacher. He would ask students to move out and then bring them back to the class in just 02-03 minutes. He had excused and forgiven Manpreet manier times but she was like determined to create disturbance. The class teacher went a bit harsh and asked manpreet to sit next to pushpraj in the same row. Manpreet was asked to sit with pushpraj only because he was very silent, serious for studies though not amongst the rankers and not at all talkative.

Fortunately, Manpreet was his neighbour. Her house was just 50-60 meters away from Pushpraj's. They used to go to school together. As said she was very naughty, she didn't stop her conduct. I mean misconducts. She sustained creating disturbance and doing all nuisance things inside the class that would rage the class teacher.

Pushpraj was truly an innocent boy who didn't know about love, means GF–BF love. And this girl Manpreet was trying her best to spoil pushpraj by drowning him in love case scenarios and then what? The day she was asked to sit with him, she started drawing broken hearts and write P and M by dissecting from the middle (P for Pushpraj and M for herself i.e. Manpreet). She used to draw it all over in his notebooks. Pushpraj used to cut them all but could not erase as they were all drawn by pen, sketch pens etc.... On every drawing, pushpraj stopped her and cut her all the hearts drawn in his notebook.

He didn't know the meaning of those hearts drawn in his notebook as he had never been to such scenario before. Pushpraj only knew that the hearts drawn were drawings, which is drawn either in sketch book or drawing book. He said manier times to Manpreet and requested her not to spoil the notebook and always suggested her to draw it in drawing or sketch book. But she didn't stop. However, he also said, he would complain to her father but that hardly brought change in her conduct. She was incorrigible seriously as she kept on drawing hearts, writing P & M inside it. And Pushpraj's job was to cut, cross and when the page was full, then tear that out and throw. Pushpraj couldn't understand the objective of Manpreet's conduct and he felt very disappointed about his notebooks which were used for drawing hearts by Manpreet. This is what he only knew.

Ramesh his Chum & Best friend had solutions for all such cases. He was like love GURU and was famous for resolving such scenarios. It was January 1996, when pushpraj explained him the entire scene and showed him his all notebooks having hearts drawn all over. Ramesh was never serious for studies but if somebody talked about love case scenarios. One could see and sense a deep seriousness within him. He listened the entire scenario first silently and curiously. All of sudden, he started smiling and patting Pushpraj on his right shoulder. Pushpraj was happy seeing Ramesh smiling as he became confident and was ready to listen something good from Ramesh.

Ramesh asked Pushpraj about Dilwale Dulhaniya Le Jayenge (DDLJ) movie. He asked whether Pushpraj had watched the movie or not? Luckily it was the last and recent movie which he had watched at that time which was released in Oct. 1995. He started linking Raj (the Actor-DDLJ) with Pushpraj and Simran (The Actress-DDLJ) with Manpreet. He said to Pushpraj that love is breeding inside Manmeet's heart & soul and she considers Pushpraj like Raj and herself like Simran. Ramesh strictly advised and suggested Pushpraj to start doing the same which she does in his notebook. And now what, lessons of Ramesh were being followed and implemented by Pushpraj. Pushpraj, now started drawing hearts in her note book. But those hearts drawn were cut and were subjected to rejection and dismissal. Manpreet had stopped drawing hearts in his notebook and it was only Pushpraj who continued but was rejected and no more appreciated. She strictly and angrily said she would complain about it to the class teacher. Pushpraj was recognized as the most sincere student of the class and was honored a pen by him. He didn't want to project a negative display of himself so he stopped drawing hearts and felt disappointed.

Pushpraj was shocked and flabbergasted as he wanted to know, what went wrong? The girl who was drawing hearts in his notebook and did that for almost 8-10 days stopped drawing? And this only happened after meeting Ramesh. He wanted to know. He again approached Ramesh and shared his dreadful, sorrowful scene happened with him. This time Ramesh didn't smile but laughed. Pushpraj was in dilemma, was a bit ambiguous about Ramesh's expression as maximum knew his smile meant good news and laughter a bad one or something which he didn't want to listen. He was shocked when Ramesh said Time and Tides wait for none. This was a pet line which was always said by the class teacher whenever he would see student's non serious and wasting time. Ramesh said; it was an open opportunity so he himself started drawing hearts in her notebook and write M/S and Manpreet took of the same by writing S/M. The best friend Ramesh remained no more his best friend but only for a week. As they sustained their friendship when Manpreet got associated with Hariya. This is how Pushpraj started his career in love case scenario. He had some memorable and funny experiences in school life and cherished whenever thought of.

5

DISCRIMINATION EMERGED SINGER

Pushpraj completed his Xth in 1999 from the best school of town. Now he had to take up his 10+2 and there was no English medium school offering 10 + 2. He had no option as the family was under financial crisis due to which he couldn't move to Harinagar to take up 10 + 2.

His father always tried his best to provide his kids the best education but this time for Pushpraj after 10th for 10 + 2 became difficult. Poor Economic condition didn't allow Pushpraj to study in a school where he wanted. Finally, his father had got his admission done in the school where he worked as a sweeper. He took admission and he chose Biology. He was a regular student and attended classes daily. It didn't have a co-education format. It was a boy's college. However, Pushpraj was happy to study in the school where his father worked.

Pushpraj started going to school to attend lectures. Sometimes he went with his father and had watched him sweeping the class rooms, offices, corridors and then collecting all rags and putting them on fire. It was truly very sad for Pushpraj to see his father work so harder, sweat like anything, having mouth & face covered to avoid dust, picking rags from all over the college. But Mr. Father never asked his kids to help him out in his work. Though his kids wanted and sometimes they did but Mr. Father stopped them and always said; that was not their place. They have to prove themselves to be the best sons of this world by achieving success and taking their parents name at a great height. The love, the learnings that Pushpraj had from his Mom & dad were the best gift which he has. We are taught to expect unconditional love from our parents which he got. The depth of the love of his parents cannot be measured. It was like no other relationship. It exceeded concern for one's life.

Pushpraj's one goal was very clear: to be true to his parents and family as loyal son, as a caring brother, as a loving brother to sister and of course a good human being.

Pushpraj was from a family which was suffering financial crisis but it doesn't mean, his childhood suffered. He wouldn't say it. It helped him grow up. He stayed out of trouble. He was never surrounded or armed by any problems. His parents taught him what's wrong and right.

It was winter season, when he was in XIth standard. Pushpraj was attending chemistry in class and then entered English teacher to announce the date of an event which was scheduled on Basant Panchami. English teacher shared the lists of the activities which he wanted students to perform on that day. It was 2 in 1 event means Annual function along with Basant Panchami. There were several competitions like: Dance, Singing, Painting, Rangoli etc.... Students were asked to register their names for the competition as per their choice. Pushpraj was rejoicing like anything. He was glad and happy. I am sure you would remember in previous chapter that Pushpraj was good in extracurricular activities.

He chose singing and decided to perform a patriotic song. He chose singing as his father had Brass Band Baaja which people used to book for wedding, Engagement, death for all the occasions. Mostly, people hired Brass Band for wedding and Death to carry wedding procession and Death procession respectively. In wedding, all joyful songs and in death procession just one track does the needful and that is "Raghupati Raghav Raja Ram, Patit Pawan Sita Ram". This is sung only in death occasions however these are true lines which should be sung and played in all occasions but people prefer it on one's final journey after life i.e. death.

Talking about his Brass Band, he had a Band trolley on which Singer stood up along with a Casio player and sometimes a Trumpet player and remaining were standing down having 5-6 Brass, 3-4 trumpets, drums and 2 side drums, 2 Jhunjhunas (percussion) & a Big size drum to bring base in the rhythm. So he chose singing as he knew he would get a kind a preparation from the Brass Band. But unfortunately, he couldn't get any prep as it was the wedding season and almost Brass Band was occupied throughout till mid of March. Mostly his father used to get out stationed bookings.

Pushpraj's mother took of the charge. His mother said Pushp you sing in front of me as if you are auditioning yourself in front of a Music judge as like participants do in singing reality show. She remembered a Singing reality show format. So, his mother became judge and judged him, used to correct him where ever she felt the loop hole. His mother used to close her eyes and feel the lines of the song. Pushpraj in those 3-4 days would have sung for more than 100 times a day and that too in front of her mother and his mother would curiously and carefully listen to rectify and correct him wherever he would go wrong.

His mother observed the improvement and betterment in the song flow. She explained him the meaning and sense of all the 4 paragraphs that the song had so that he brings the exact feel and gives the appropriate touch to it. My God! Mother's love, the unconditional love for Pushpraj was amazing. He used to sing in kitchen and she would listen. Sometimes, while cleaning the house, she herself asked him to sing. She worked harder only because she loved him unconditionally and her love didn't expect anything from him. His mother used to teach her kids a lesson, "Give your 100% without bothering for results, you fail or win that's not that important. What is important is that you don't give up if you fail. As those who don't give up are the super winners. Important is don't be egoistic or proud, if you win. Be down to earth always as you were before. Celebrate your victory with all". She worked harder on Pushpraj's singing as she wanted him to feel that he did his 100% and he made his true effort for the same and lest should not feel disappointed or demoralized if he doesn't win. She was a great teacher, a great motivator and a great friend.

Pushpraj had wonderful time with his mother in his childhood. He always cherished a moment when his mother would feed him food and he would sing. My God! His mother had great patience. She would listen him singing and saying Chotu (Nick name-Pushpraj); Eat first then sing to me. Singing while eating is not a good habit as it can choke the throat. But Pushpraj never listened. He continued. Rice and pulse mixed together along with vegetable or chutney (sauce) was fed patiently to Pushpraj for more than an hour. Pushpraj was just 17 of his age and he always loved to be fed by his mother.

Preparation was done and Mrs. Mother had confidence about his victory. She said him that he is her "Best Singer" and she is a "fan" of him. Now he grew up confidently for the performance. He was happy to know that he has a fan following and the first fan he had was his loving mother, his world, his everything. The final day arrived.......

It was very cold outside as it was January. That day had almost zero visibility. The surrounding was armed and surrounded by dense fog. He had shower. He went to the room where his father had shop (Brass Band shop) and they used to call it as Baja wala kamra. This room had a temple where idles of Gods & Goddesses were kept.

Pushpraj was a strong devotee of goddess Saraswati, and that day was Basant Panchami when students offer prayer and wish to gain wisdom for their better future and career. He offered prayer by chanting saraswati Mantra which is mainly chanted to seek blessings to eradicate the evils of ignorance and bestow the devotee with intelligence. After offering prayer, he asked his mother to give him a small Ruby (Lal Chunri). He kept goddess Saraswati's small idol in Ruby and wrapped idle inside it and kept in his shirts pocket. Before leaving for the school, he sang the song again in front of his mother to gain confidence. He touched her feet, took the blessings, suited himself on Red color Hero cycle one size smaller than the bigger one and reached school.

He saw a huge crowd inside the Pandaal (A temporary platform set up for the event using Tent materials). There were many stalls inside and outside selling food items, cloth, handicraft, stationery items. The Saraswati Mantra was set on the track due to which no body was able to listen other's talk. And in the mid, technicians were checking the sound system and saying "Hello Microphone Check, 1, 2, 3". Orchestra people were setting up their instruments. Pushpraj had arrived early, he reached at around 08:30 AM and the program was scheduled from 09:00 AM onwards. He met his friends, had chit chat and then he went far away from the crowd to find a silent place. Though he couldn't find as the sound was set louder and was creating kind of disturbance. He was determined to win and to deliver his best. He took the Goddess Saraswati's Idle out from his pocket, unwrapped, and took that in his both the hands. He bowed in front of her by bringing Goddesses' feet in contact with his head. He closed his eyes and started singing as if he was singing before his mother. He gained confidence like anything and he knew, he was going to be the best and be winner that day but future had something else in store for him. He was going to be discriminated. He was going to face disappointment. He was going to be demoralized the same day only because he was a "SON OF A SWEEPER". He was about to meet an unfavorable circumstance.....

People say "Always Do your best" but scenario with Pushpraj was different. Discrimination between Rich & poor, Sweeper's son and others, Discrimination between tallest and wretched. However, he didn't know the consequences.

"Ya Kundendu Tushorahara Dhavala Ya Shubhra Vastravita

Ya Veena Varadanda Manditakara Ya Shveta Padmasana

Ya Brahmachyuta Shankara Prabhritibihi Devaih Sada Pujita

Sa Man Pattu Saravatee Bhagavatee Nihshesha Jadyapala".

With these shlokas, English teacher began the event. All chief guest, special guests and invitees almost had marked their presence. There was a very big stage beautifully decorated with flowers and good lightings. The function started, the chief guest was asked to offer flowers to Goddess Saraswati and to share few words to students for their better career growth. The Chief Guest ended by wishing participants Good luck. Program, first started with dance then drama and then the last was singing.

Pushpraj normally used to have 8-10 paranthas (fried form of chapati) with Aaloo tamatar ki sabzi (potato-tomato vegetable) and have them with Black Tea by dipping into it. But that day he just had one parantha with Tea only. Program started at 10:15 AM and continued till 05:30 PM in the evening. Dancing was over, than drama. That too finished. Finally the last program was singing and the time was 03:00 PM. He waited throughout. He was hungry. His stomach was aching but determined to perform and to give his best. One after the other the participants were called and he would see their performances. He was curious and he was expecting that the next name would be his after a participant finished his performance. Manoj, Sukhram, Pappu and many names were called. Just one name was missing or else it was not called. Program finished and names of the winners were being called. Now he realized he will not be allowed to give his best as he was discriminated and became a victim of discrimination in the hands of Cruel, Inhuman discriminators. He was discriminated only because he was son of a Sweeper.

He ran away from there and kept running in the ground, singing the song loudly in pain. He was crying badly and madly as his tears was not stopping. He knew he was discriminated. It was not the first time that he was subjected to it. He had been discriminated before as well. There were few who used to consider him and his family wretched. There were few who called Pushpraj

"Bajaniyahwa ka launda" (Abusing way to say son of Band Man) an abusive way which held him down whenever he listened. But he was determined to be cheerful and happy in whatever circumstance he may find himself. For he had learned that the greater part of our misery or unhappiness was determined not by our circumstance but by our disposition. The most important lesson that he learned was to trust his Mom, Dad, Siblings and God in every circumstances.

The instance he reached back home. He went to his mother and said in teary eyes that he was not called and allowed to perform. He was sobbing badly, painfully as he practiced harder for it. The mother was also crying but couldn't shed her tears out. She just kissed him and said "never mind you will definitely become a great singer one day". He cried almost whole day. Mother said that she is going to kitchen and will prepare omelet for him as he was hungry whole day. Mother went to the kitchen and she was chopping onion sitting down on the floor. He too went to the kitchen as he wanted bread as well with the omelet. Before he could say anything he saw teary eyes of her mother, eyes downcast and completely lost and forgetful. They were not the water drops that rolled out due to chopping onion. But it was her pain, love, and care for Pushpraj which rolled out as tears from her eyes. He had always seen his mother in pain which she never displayed to anyone. Pushpraj was back to swing as the entire family empathized him and he knew that he was blessed with the best loving family whose love, care and everything was true. He took a firm determination that he would show everybody his singing talent. He moved on.

6

FINALLY A SINGER

It is said "the harder the struggle, the more glorious the triumph". Pushpraj didn't give up, he stayed focused, positive and strong. In the same year. When he was in 10 + 2 he went for CATC (Combined Annual Training Camp) A 12 day SCOUT training program which was held in HARINAGAR. There were approx. 50-60 candidates from his college and a gathering of almost 2000 + SCOUT cadets who came from different Battalions. Pushpraj was CQMS in his battalion (Company Quarter Master Sergeant), It was an SCOUT Rank which he held. The best thing about being a CQMS was he will not do guards, nor perform the duties of under officer (V.O.) or Senior under officer (S.U.O) unless specially ordered by A.S.O. (Associate SCOUT officer. This Rank had few more responsibilities where in pushpraj had to perform all like-he was responsible for the cleanliness of cook houses, latrines, etc. The good thing was he did not guard at nights. Guarding at night is a tough job.

Pushpraj and everybody were getting up by 04:30 AM and by 05:30 AM the commanding officers; A.N.O's expected their gathering in the ground, battalion wise. They had to run for more than 5 kilometers every day. Sit ups, push-ups and this used to happen till 06:30 AM. Again they were expected for gathering in the ground for further Training. Here everybody was a cadet. Didn't know which family did one come from? What was the family background? He truly enjoyed and was happy enough to see the equality not discrimination. All were equally treated as a Cadet. No discrimination, no bias nothing just all were cadets and that was the identification they all had there in SCOUT training. Training was tough but it taught him the lessons of duty, unity and discipline.

It was the 10th day of CATC training and cadets were asked to register their names for cultural activities. There had activities like singing, dancing, acting, and singing had two categories. Solo singing and group. He got his name registered for solo singing which was about to happen in next 2 days, means the 12th day (last day of training). He decided to sing the same song which he chose to perform there in his school on Basant Panchami day where he was not allowed only because he was SON of a sweeper.

Nainsukh, his friend was good in dholak. Though there was no dholak. But he used plastic bucket and played that as dholak. He was really good in it. Pushpraj requested him if he could give him a prep on rhythm. As there had an Orchestra on the last day to play Music (background) on all the performances. He agreed and Pushpraj started rehearsing but only at nights and he did it for 02 days only. He wanted to speak to his mother and wanted to sing in front of her and make his voice listen to her mother over phone. But alas, there was no phone at his home. Mobile technology at that time was not heard. He was tormenting like anything to sing to her but that could not happen. Nainsukh was very helpful and supportive as he supported Pushpraj for his singing and wanted him to win. Nainsukh didn't know about his melodious voice but later after listening his singing talent he was confident about Pushpraj's win.

The 12th day and Pushpraj was set to win. He suited himself for the victory. He just had a threat of being discriminated. There had an Auditorium. Cadets got their seats. Surrounding was noisy. Sound system was being organized. Participants were found busy preparing for their performances. There were few who were practicing singing loudly at the back stage and few singing in wash room. Few combing their hair, applying cream, tucking shirt and did everything which would turn them good looking. Pushpraj was seated in 5th row and on 08th seat from the left corner. The program was inaugurated by Mr. Commanding Officer (C.O.) and then performance started. Everybody was doing great and performing their best. Watching others performances, Pushpraj was getting nervous. But his nervousness didn't know that his performance was going to overpower and gain confidence. The stage didn't know that it was going to give birth to a singer. The audience didn't know that it's the day of that SWEEPER'S SON. Pushpraj's name was called. He was shivering. He made his way to the stage. Nervousness was overpowering him. Huge crowed was generating fear factor within his heart and soul. He came before Microphone, Checked his voice by slightly humming the song that he prepared for the day. He couldn't maintain Eye contact with anybody. His eyes were downcast and looked only to the microphone remembering his mother and that day when he was discriminated.

But he was determined this time as he had to win. He had no option. He knew that SUCCESS is the only option". He touched his forehead and throat. Took the Ad lib along with Alap. "Whistles, round of Applaud,

Pushpraj, Pushpraj, Pushpraj" his team cheered by taking his name. Enthusiasm, Excitement, Zeal turned his nervousness into confidence. He held his head up and maintained intense Eye contact. And then sang with full passion and determination beautifully.

Yes, it was his day. The stage was set on fire when he performed and everybody knew; that was the best performance and decided him to declare the winner. Undoubtedly, his name was called with excitement, respect and was invited to come on stage. He was called, "and son of a SWEEPER was a Singer now". He received his Medal and became the title winner.

The Battalion was very happy. They were rejoicing and that plastic bucket was played in such a great excitement by Nainsukh that it broke from the base.

It's not just the medal that Pushpraj won but he won hearts of many as now 2000 + people knew him and his singing talent. It was a pride and honor for him as nobody had ever grabbed any medal in SCOUT for the school. It was Pushpraj, the SON OF A SWEEPER who gave recognition to himself and of course to the school as well. Pushpral was a SINGER now. And gradually he kept up the pace and bagged 02 medals and 18 awards in singing. He didn't give up and became a "SUPER WINNER".

7

PUSHPRAJ MISSING. BAGGED JOB

He was missing from his home for almost 02 months. Nobody knew about him and where he was. Many considered him dead and many said may be kidnapped. His family was under depression. It was like a mournful situation for his family. Everybody released hope and gave up saying Pushpraj would never come back. He would be no more by now.

He ran away from his home after a year of completion of 10 + 2 as in to work and to provide financial support to his family so that his younger ones don't face any compromise and they are able to do that they desire. He ran away from his house as he wanted to be a doctor but he couldn't only because the family was under financial crisis and were badly hit by poverty. He didn't inform anybody as he knew that had he informed, he would had never allowed going outside the town for work. Pushpraj at 18 years was grown up and quite matured. He knew he had to work and support his family. He got determined and ran away from house stealing Rs. 435 from his father's KURTA. It was 04:45 PM and the train was at 05:15 PM. He had nothing with him just a pen and a small diary and then moved out of the house to board the train and experience the new phase of life, the struggling part of life. He boarded the train and took a seat for Hari nagar. Train almost took 3.5 hours to reach Hari nagar. Continuously for 3.5 hours, Pushpraj was thinking about work that what kind of job he can land in? And will somebody give him a job? He was just 10 + 2, had no computer skills as computer was like a dream for him. He had never touched computer before. He decided he will work in a hotel as a waiter, helper, sweeper or whatever job is available. His objective was just to earn money and to provide financial support to his family that's it.

He reached Hari nagar and when he walked out of the railway station he saw a man fixing posters on walls. The posters were displaying information about a call center job in Roshananbad. And the salary was 08-10 thousand. He was very happy after reading information from the poster. Pushpraj then approached to those men who were fixing the posters. He asked those men about the job, salary, location and few more details. Those men told Pushpraj to move to Roshanabad and attend an interview which was scheduled just the next day of his arrival to Hari nagar. He was happy and he was told in such a way as if he would easily get a job there.

He went back to the station. Enquired about trains going to Roshanabad. He got to know about an express train whose arrival was scheduled somewhere at around 23:30 hr. Pushpraj went to the window counter, purchased ticket for Roshanabad. He was there at platform No.1, where he was waiting for the train. He was still in dilemma about Roshanabad movement. His heart and soul had so many questions for him like what kind of job is a call centre job. Will he be allowed to work there? How will be the people? He didn't know that he had to face interview and for that he would require C.V. He had no idea that's it's a corporate job. He just knew he was going to find a job and work.

Train arrived, it was late by 30-40 minutes. He boarded the sleeper coach and saw darkness inside the coach. He felt may be passengers were sleeping. He found seat. He didn't know that sleeper class was a reserved coach for which passengers carry a reservation ticket. He didn't know about reservation system as his area had (Meter Gauge train) Choti line train where passengers were allowed to sit anywhere, wherever they wished. The seat just next to the door was partially occupied by Pushpraj by sitting on the edge of the birth as there was a man who was sleeping. The passenger who was sleeping in the birth got up as his legs sensed inconvenience at his lower. He got up and said that, birth belonged to him as he had got that reserved. Pushpraj answered that he too had ticket for Roshanabad and he won't disturb him.

Passenger asked Pushpraj to move out of the sleeper coach as that was a reservation coach and ticket that Pushpraj had was a General ticket and he was not entitled to travel in the coach where he entered. The train was moving. He had no option. Pushpraj asked the passenger about the General Coach's position. He came to know that was just after the Engine but he couldn't go to the General Coach as train was moving. He got up from the seat and stood at the door and waited for the next station to de board to get in a General Coach.

Surajpur was the station where he had to change the coach but he didn't know that in next 05 minutes he was going to be fined by T.T.E. for traveling in Reservation Coach with a General Ticket. A constable having Torch arrived with a T.T.E. and asked Pushpraj about the ticket. The constable asked for ticket to Pushpraj. Pushpraj was afraid of as he knew he was traveling on an inappropriate ticket. He gave the ticket to the constable and constable gave to the T.T.E. T.T.E. said that it was not a valid ticket to travel and so Pushpraj had to pay fine of Rs. 50/- else he would be taken behind bars. Pushpraj had never faced such scenarios before. The moment he was told that he would be prisoned. He didn't give any thought and he paid Rs. 50/- to the T.T.E though he was not given any berth but he was permitted to travel in the same coach. Pushpraj was left up with Rs. 210/-. He slept sitting on the train's floor just next to the wash basin.

Roshanabad arrived at around 06:30 AM. The place where he had to go was Mainawati Marg. He came out of the Railway Station and asked the way to reach Mainawati Marg. As the office was situated in Mainawati

Marg. He reached Mainawati Marg very early perhaps the time was 07:00 AM. He saw a public toilet and he thought of getting fresh. He saw huge rush out there. He saw people dressing up, organizing folders, suiting in formals. He asked them about the rush to a person who had a tie but didn't know how to prepare knot. He was struggling and trying his best to prepare knot. Pushpraj went to him and asked if he could help him out for the tie. Pushpraj prepared knot and fastened it to the collar. He was thanked by that person. Pushpraj asked him about his formal attire and also asked what was he preparing for? That person said he was going to appear for an interview in A Hotel, at Nirvana Marg, Roshanabad and the profile was of a Call Center Executive. Pushpraj was happy enough as he too came for the same profile but not for this company. He asked whether he could apply or not? Anybody can apply that man said. So, Pushpraj decided to appear for the Interview. He requested that man, if he could wait and take him to the venue along with him. He was kind enough and agreed to wait.

Pushpraj went for shower. He did not have towel. Neither clothes to change nor tooth paste. He used his finger to clean his teeth. He was not having any cloth to change. He had no towel. He took off his vest (inner wear on top) and had shower. After having shower he used his vest to clean and dry his body and wore the vest back again. His appearance was disheveled as his clothes were dirty. He moved on along with that man to get interviewed. Everybody was submitting their CVs to the receptionist but Pushpraj didn't have such documents to submit. He didn't want to miss the interview and the time was 09:00 AM. The interview was scheduled from 10:00 AM onwards. He asked to the person for creating CV whom he helped preparing tie. He said that Pushpraj should find a cyber café and should request to the café owner to help him get a CV.

He struggled harder but he couldn't find any shop as it was very early for the shops to open. Finally, at 10:20 AM, he found a person cleaning shop and luckily that was a cyber café and he was the owner. The café owner took 25 minutes to organize his counter. He offered prayer and then he asked Pushpraj to share his details and qualifications only, as rest he would manage by himself. He took 05 minutes and Pushpraj's CV was ready. It was 11:00 AM now. He paid him Rs. 40/- and rushed to the hotel for the Interview. Finally he submitted his CV to the receptionist.

He was directed to a hall that had a big gathering. Everybody was looking comely except him. All were well dressed, groomed but Pushpraj's appearance was completely untidy. He was very nervous as he was confident about his dismissal. There was an Interviewer who was calling names one by one and was asking candidates to introduce themselves being at their place. Pushpraj didn't know about introduction format. He started observing the introductions of the applicants keenly to get a better idea to understand the format and delivery.

Pushpraj, can you tell us something about yourself? Interviewer asked, as it was his turn. He nervously answered. He just said his name and the place where he came from. That's it and was silent. Interviewer expected him to speak a bit more about him but he couldn't. No more questions were asked to him. That was the elimination round and he didn't know. He was disqualified saying he should work communication. Pushpraj had a new learning as he came across his grey areas where he needed to work as in to win over such interviews. He didn't give up and he decided to put up there in Roshanabad until he had bagged a job.

He had Rs. 75/- only and he knew putting up in Roshanabad with Rs. 75/- is impossible. He had to work and so he started searching work. He approached and found a DHABA. There was a man who was standing near tandoor preparing Chapati. Pushpraj approached him and requested if he could keep him on work. He said to Pushpraj that it's not a big deal to give him a work but he should talk to the dhaba Owner. Pushpraj approached the owner and begged to keep him on work. He agreed and said he would pay Rs. 700/- a month but the good thing was food and accommodation was free. He had to sleep there in the Dhaba only but he never had a sound sleep as it was a highway Dhaba and vehicles were very frequently visiting the dhaba. He worked there for 22 days.

He used to get up early morning by 04:00 AM and then take all the huge vessels under the hand pump to clean. It was consuming 30 minutes minimum to clean the vessels and the utensils. Post cleaning the utensils he had to broom the Dhaba and then mop. Cleaning, mopping, serving food and sometimes chopping vegetables and cutting, were his daily routine. He never dreamt, that a day he will be doing such kind of work. Not even a single moment he forgot his parents, his siblings. He loved her mother very much. He used to cry all day long thinking about his mother's love because he never expected this coming across his way. There was a time when his mother's hand would come forward to serve him food and

Then she would give head massage and he would fall asleep. This for him became a dream as there was nobody to care for him.

He was very firm determined and he knew his grey areas and it was communication where he had to work on. Whenever he had time he would watch English films, news channels and was trying to imitate their mouth movements so that his communication is enhanced. He was hardly getting time but he used to practice a lot. He used to keep English newspaper to read. He used to read them loudly whenever alone and sometimes murmur when customers around or anybody there. Once a day there was a terrific rain. It rained like cats and dogs. It was muddy all over and floor was highly slippery. It was afternoon when three customers arrived. Before they could order, he was asked to serve 3 glass water on the table. He was walking very slowly as he knew if he does not walk carefully he would fall. And when he reached closer to the table, very close to the table, the instance he tried to keep those glasses on the table, he slipped, fell down and broke his jaws. Unfortunately, water got spilled on two of them. They became angry and they used all those abusive words that one would never like to listen, even imagine in thoughts. There was one who slapped badly to Pushpraj and he fell down again and the other one clobbered him on his back by elbow by using abusive words to him. The workers came and requested those customers to leave him.

They asked sorry to those customers on Pushpraj's behalf. That day he cried all day long. He was never abused before the way he was abused that day. His mother, father, sister, brothers everyone was abused due to his mistake. He could not forgive himself. He loved his family a lot and they were being abused. He was like in trauma. Pushpraj was requesting them–"Don't hit, please don't abuse, He felt sorry". He was groaning loudly in pain but they did not listen him just kept thrashing him. He was bleeding badly. And he broke his jaws by colliding to the table.

At home, in school, several times Pushpraj had bled during games, minor accidents and it was first her mother who would come in teary eyes looking impatiently to the cuts or injuries as if she had bled, her heart bled and ask infinite questions. It was her mother's unconditional love that she wiped the blood with her pallu (long trailing part of the saree) and then bandaged tearing a part of pallu to cover the cuts and asking him that should she prepare PARANTHA & BLACK TEA? And then she used to go to the kitchen hugging her kid..... This was her mother. He missed her mother a lot. He loved her a lot. She was his lifeline. He cried, his heart cried whole day long.

It was almost going to be a month about his missing from home. He wanted to tell to his parents but only once he had landed in a job. He worked there for 22 days (At Dhaba). The very 22nd day he came to know about an interview for marketing profile in Nayagaon. He got interviewed and finally got placed for Rs. 6300/- a month. He had to move to Nayagaon for his job. He had to join at the earliest.. He had time for almost 7-8 days. He told about his job to the Dhaba owner and also asked him to pay his remuneration. He payed him the remuneration and gave Rs. 300/- extra. He gave his blessings to Pushpraj and wished him good luck.

Pushpraj suited himself, boarded the train having general ticket and reached Nayagaon.

Pushpraj joined the company and started working but he had no place to put up as he was penniless. He was serving office for 09 hours and after office he was picking up rags, garbage all day long from Railway stations, Bus stops, Streets, Dump yard to manage bread for himself. He kept his pain aside; he was thinking only about his family, he was thinking about helping his family. His goal was clear to him as he wanted to bring smile on his parents face and that smile would be noble earning for him which would give his efforts a meaning. Who would do such jobs? I mean entering in Drains, picking up plastic materials by putting your hands, your legs inside it and that too just to make 70-80 rupees. This particular job 'means' Rag picking makes ones appearance disheveled and dirty but the job is neither disheveled nor dirty because that is the first step for pushpraj turning him to Professional from that Rag Picker and Dhaba servant. As mentioned he was penniless that is why he was putting up sometimes at Footpath, sometimes Railway Stations or at Bus stops. He was making approx. 70-80 rupees a day and he would spend the earned amount wisely to avoid inconvenience that could arrive anytime. He continued that for 19 days and post 19 days he managed permanent shelter for himself.

Somebody has said: "YOU MAY NOT BE THE STRONGEST, YOU MAY NOT BE THE FASTEST, and BUT YOU WILL BE DAMNED IF YOU ARE NOT TRYING YOUR HARDEST"

Talking about Pushpraj: He is a man of determination defining the true meaning of determination. "He is a man who designed his own destiny and he is the AUTHOR of his life" We all should get determined to face struggles to be a HERO like PUSHPRAJ.

After 18 days of work his month completed and he received his salary for Rs.3780/- He went to a P.C.O. (Public Calling Office) and dialed a telephone number of a telegram office near to his house. He spoke to TAAR CHACHA (care taker of Telegram office) and requested him to put his father on line as in to speak to him. TAAR chacha told Pushpraj about the condition of his family. He came to know about her mother who was dying for him, expecting him to come back home and give her a hug and ask Pushpraj to promise that he would never do such acts again. Father who was just silent and was not speaking to anyone. There were many who left up their hopes saying "Pushpraj would have died. He is no more". He would have committed suicide. When he listened all these from Taar chacha, tears rolled out from his eyes and expressed curiosity to talk to his family that right moment. He was asked to call back after 40 minutes. He called back and then it was his father who picked up the phone and he was crying as he had sensed the sighs of his father. With teary eyes Pushpraj said "PAPA" and the tears rolled out from his eyes too and was gasping, sobbing which did not allow him to speak for a minute. Pushpraj's father said "GHAR AA JAO BETA" (come back home, my son). Pushpraj said he will definitely come in "HOLI". He asked father about his mother first, whom he loved the most and then asked about his siblings. He said his father that he had landed in a job and he had got his salary today. He said, He has started working and he is sending Money order of Rs. 1000/- to his father. He also said that he would send money every month to his house. Since then, Pushpraj started supporting his family. He understood his responsibility at a very kinder age. He understood his role in his family for his dear ones.

Pushpraj knew nothing was impossible. He knew the difference between the impossible and the possible lied in a person's determination. His dream was not to get a job but to avoid and negate the unfavorable circumstances which were ready to come in his sibling's career like a hindrance. Someone has said;

"Devote yourself to an idea.

8

IN LOVE WITH JYOTSNA.

S omebody has said, "Love and death are two uninvited guests, when they will come nobody knows, But both do the same work, one takes heart and the other one takes its beats. And sometimes love takes both heart and the beats".....

He crossed all the boundaries for Jyotsna (his beloved).

Broke all the chains that did not allow him to have Jyotsna.

Was clobbered, thrashed but determined to have her in life,

He chose to be defamed, lost image only to have Jyotsna.

But couldn't have, he failed to have her,

He smiled and left himself to die for Jyotsna.

He was a Center Manager/Business Development Manager in an organization at Harinagar. He was never fallen in love before. He didn't know that love was just about to arrive and take entry in his life.

Once a day he planned to visit Sudarshanganj. He didn't know that his soul would meet its soul mate. He didn't know that he would fall in love at first sight and that's what happened. He visited a Buddha temple in Sudarshanganj which is lord Buddha's Monastery. He was inside a temple where he was touching prayer wheels which is said to bring great purification to negative karmas and peace to your inner soul. And yes may be that day his soul was about to get peace. Pushpraj was in deep prayer when a yellow color tippet slightly hit his face and broke his concentration. "I am sorry" was said by the girl who too was touching the prayer wheels. Pushpraj didn't even know that the girl walking ahead and touching prayer wheels was her soul-mate. He didn't respond to her apology as he was lost. He started feeling a kind of commotion in his heart. And his heart as if was forcing him to talk and to get her within his heart and soul. The place was fully crowded. He searched for the girl there till evening 06:00 pm but he didn't find. He felt very disappointed and demoralized. He tried his best. He visited all the temples out there but he couldn't find. He went back to Harinagar with a ray of hope that he would find her someday, somehow. Pushpraj decided to visit Sudarshanganj every weekend i.e. Saturdays and Sundays until he finds her. He started visiting Sudarshanganj every weekend to find her and luckily after a month he saw her in the same yellow color tippet.

"Hi!" Pushpraj said to her. She too said "Hi" but frowningly. "You remember, your tippet came on my face a month ago while touching prayer wheels"- Pushpraj said. She said "yes" she remembered and she also said "SORRY" about it. By the way my name is Pushpraj-Pushpraj said, she said; ok but In return she didn't tell her name. Pushpraj asked "May I know your name please"? "Jyotsna", she said her name was "Jyotsna" and then what he was lost listening such a beautiful name and said "Wow" that's truly a nice name.... They both were touching prayer wheel and Pushpraj had curiosity to know more about Jyotsna. What did she do? Where was she from? And most important thing what was her contact number? So that he keeps a touch base with her.....

Pushpraj asked about her work. She said; she was English language trainer. She taught spoken English for part time in Harinagar. Pushpraj was more than happy to listen this from her because he required an English language trainer for full time for the organization he was working. He didn't give any thought to it. He directly asked to Jyotsna, will she be interested to work with a renowned organization famous across the world as an English language Trainer, for full time? Jyotsna said; "Yes" and he was like on top of the world. His happiness was like he got treasure. "Shall we go for coffee to discuss job details and the compensation"? Pushpraj said to Jyotsna. "Yes", Jyotsna replied. Pushpraj didn't want to lose her, so the instance they reached to restaurant.

He asked for her mobile number. It was very unusual for Jyotsna about Pushpraj asking contact number. At least he should have placed the order for coffee, made light chat but no, he directly jumped for the contact number. However, Jyotsna shared her number to him though she didn't want to but she did. While having coffee, they shared their family details, hobbies, like, dislikes and lot many things. And the most important thing which he wanted to ask was about her boyfriend but he asked it indirectly. He asked her;

Pushpraj: What does your husband do?

Jyotsna: I am unmarried.

Pushpraj: When are you getting married?

Jyotsna: Have no plans as if now.

Pushpraj: That's good. You want to be independent first, right?

Jyotsna: It's not like that. I mean if I get someone better in life. May be I would stop and get him in life.

Pushpraj: That's really nice. Let's meet tomorrow in Harinagar.

Jyotsna: Yeah sure, what time do you want me to be there?

Pushpraj: At 11:30 AM, will that be fine? Will have lunch together to discuss more.

Jyotsna: Sure, but what else to discuss?

Pushpraj: Salary, content, module and few more things.

Jyotsna: O.K. fine.....

Pushpraj after conversation was very happy as he knew, she had no boyfriend. The whole day he was drowned in her thought. He was preparing for next day as she would come to office. He wanted to talk her over phone but what to talk? He had no genuine reason. He kept dialing her mobile number on phone and then was cancelling. Dial and then cancel, he did this whole night but couldn't dare to dial and speak to her. That night was a restless night for him. That was the start of love which had kicked his heart and started beating on her name i.e. Jyotsna. Love began and it began with a smile.... He didn't know that it would end in tears and meet dead end later. Love began in a moment, grew over time but didn't last for eternity after 21 months. But love began and started breeding within his heart and soul.....

He went to Krishna temple to offer prayer and to make a wish that Jyotsna joins for full time. He took his bike and then headed for office without breakfast. He wanted to have lunch with Jyotsna as he didn't want his tummy to over shape his body which would come right after the breakfast. He wanted to look better that's it. He reached office and that was very early. He called her this time as he couldn't stop himself but the call was unanswered. He didn't call after that. He felt that calling her back to back would be a negative gesture. He felt disappointed and saddened, didn't know what to do and what not.....He was feeling restless and his mind, heart were forcing him to call back again and speak to Jyotsna. He was holding his head and his eyes were downcast and then all of sudden his phone started vibrating. He picked up the phone and guess whose call was that? It was Jyotsna's call, he picked up.....

Pushpraj:　Hi,

Jyotsna:　I am sorry, I missed the call. I was making way to Bus stop.

Pushpraj:　It's ok. I knew that you would be busy.

Jyotsna:　Will you mind, if I reach there by 10:00 A.M.

Pushpraj:　Of course not, in fact that would be a pleasure.

Jyotsna:　Thank you so much, will catch you then.

Pushpraj:　Sure, looking forward to see you.

Pushpraj was very happy now. She made her day. He was feeling rejuvenated. That was her essence which brought smile on his face.... He had nothing to do except "wait for her". He was smiling that day like anything. Everybody in the office could sense the change in him. They all wanted to know the cause behind smile and the restlessness which too was sensed by them. Khushbu, who was a receptionist, was close to him like a friend. She came to Pushpraj and asked, Is there anything special today? He replied no, not at all just looking for a candidate for hiring here for TRAINER–ENGLISH profile. Khushbu said, are you sure? It's just a hiring process nothing else then that? Pushpraj smiled; in fact he blushed and said yes, it's just for hiring. Khushbu too smiled and said, I can see that, it's just a hiring subject..... She knew that it was something more than that....

Sometimes avoiding people is a good idea. Waiting for somebody as well is a good idea though he hated waiting but he waited for Jyotsna curiously and kept his eyes stuck at the main gate. Oh! finally, she was at the gate. He saw but he wanted to pretend as if he is unaware. He immediately kept his fingers on the keyboard and started typing. Don't know, what was he doing? But very sure, he was doing nothing rather fiddling with the desktop to pretend to her he was busy and to mark a display of a higher posted official.

Don't know, he was happy and was stressed, was curious and hesitant. These feelings had never hit his heart before. He knew this was something different. That was not a common feeling. He got nervous when he knew she was going to see him but besides that he was looking forward to see her..... She came on first floor and he saw her but he was still pretending to be busy and not seen. Jyotsna approached Khushbu (the receptionist) to ask for Pushpraj and then she was directed to his cabin. She was at the door. She opened door a bit, wished Good morning and asked permission to enter..... Pushpraj got her inside the cabin and shook hand and moved out of the cabin, asking her to make herself comfortable and would join her within a minute. He was very nervous as if he had his first job interview. He didn't go anywhere; he went to the washroom because whenever he went nervous he used to go to the washroom. Khushbu was smiling seeing him and his conduct.....

I am sorry; I had an important work to take up-Pushpraj said; after returning back to his cabin from washroom.

| Pushpraj: | How are you? Hope you didn't face problem finding this place? |
| Jyotsna: | I am good. Actually, I am acquainted with the location. |

Pushpraj: That's really nice. What would you like to
            have?

Jyotsna: Nothing just water.

Pushpraj: Sure! Water and then coffee, will that be
            fine?

Jyotsna: Alright!

Pushpraj: Can I have your C.V. please?

Jyotsna: Here you are.....

And then they had formal chat and he analyzed and checked whether she would be able to train English to students or not. Pushpraj asked her to give a demo on Tense for 20-30 minutes. She was up to the mark and then Pushpraj had confidence that he was hiring a deserving candidate.

He requested her to join for lunch and have further discussion. He asked her, her preference for the meal. She was ok with all but she said Chinese would be better. He ordered Chinese meal. Pushpraj wanted to know more about her, so he asked her about her birthday not date as the date of birth was already mentioned in her C.V. She said she was born on Wednesday. She also said she was born at 11:27 pm. He decided to surprise Jyotsna on every Wednesday. She was hired on Rs. 7500/- a month for 09 hours (09:00 AM-06:00 PM). She was fine with the salary and the joining date too as she had to join from the next day onwards. After discussion, Jyotsna asked to leave and she left at around 04:00 P.M. Jyotsna smiled; said thank you to him then shook hand and left for home.

Please don't go, stay for a while..... his heart was whispering. Please don't leave, let's sit down and chat for a while..... His heart was murmuring. And then didn't know. What had happened to him.... He ran down the stair case, reached to the main gate only to wish her "BYE". He said BYE; to her and asked her to give a call once she reaches home. She smiled and she too said "BYE"..... That was the moment when he sensed that was not common. He sensed that things were changing. He analyzed, his behavior was changing and his thoughts, brain, heart all were badly occupied by Jyotsna moments..... It is very obvious that "you just don't force love, you don't force falling in love, you don't force being in love-you just become. This had unexpectedly happened to Pushpraj. He was no more him. He was now of Jyotsna. He fell in love; he was in love with Jyotsna.....

And the love began,

She joined; they started talking every day for hours over phone. Started meeting on Sundays and on holidays only if Jyotsna had no problem or inconvenience. They knew they were getting closer day by day. They knew they were not just friends in fact more than a friend. They were like two true friends. They would share everything that they had in their mind. Moreover, they knew that they loved each other but no one broke the ice neither Pushpraj nor Jyotsna. They kept their feelings, love within their heart and soul only because they didn't want to lose their friendship. They both knew that they were in love. It's just they had to roll out their feelings in words. But it never happened..... They remained true and genuine friends.

As mentioned she was born on Wednesday. So Pushpraj had hired a restaurant which was booked for every Wednesday for an hour from 06:30–07:30 PM to celebrate her Birthday. Sometimes, Khushbu would accompany them. Pushpraj would give Jyotsna a Rose and then coffee followed by Hakka noodles and Finger fries. And then drop her to Sudarshanganj every Wednesday by his bike. Every ride was a memorable ride with her. He never wanted those rides to end as they were all the best ride of life. He wanted to ride together with her throughout life from office to his home but not as a friend, as a soul mate. Ride with her was like a miracle for him. Nothing would match in fact the simple pleasure of a bike ride with Jyotsna was unforgettable..... Sun is shining, clouds are raining or whatever, as long as he had been riding bike he knew, he was the luckiest enough to form such amazing memories and those were quality time for him. On first ride when Pushpraj asked Jyotsna to drop her to the bus stop she sat the way Indian married women sit on bike wearing saree. He said that his maternal aunt sits in the same style. And then she said, she is not Aunty and she changed the style and sat the way the bikers sit.....

They had great fun together. They really had gala time. They were enjoying life at fullest. But they were scared as well as they both knew that they were in love but they never dared to express their feelings, emotions called love. Is it true, that never hide your true feelings from someone you love? May be? But they didn't know, they kept their love locked inside their heart and soul.

9

CROSSED BOUNDARIES
FOR LOVE

L ove begins in a moment, grows over time and lasts for eternity. This did not happen with Pushpraj and Jyotsna. They had to depart and Pushpraj had to die.....

After 02 years, Pushpraj had his engagement in Bhimapur. However, he didn't want to but he had to. His heart was still beating for Jyotsna and was expecting a miracle to happen. It wanted Jyotsna to come and to say her heartiest feelings to him that she loves him.

It was a grand celebration for his family as their son was getting engaged. They had reserved bus to make way to Bhimapur from Harinagar. Pushpraj's family members, friends, relatives and Jyotsna all went to Bhimapur to attend the engagement. Everybody was enjoying, singing songs, cracking jokes, playing games but Jyotsna and Pushpraj didn't join in any of the activity. They both looked lost, tensed, sad, depressed and Jyotsna was like completely forgetful. She was never seen like that day before. They were sitting together in the bus but like strangers which never happened before..... They met as strangers and they were again strangers to each other. They both knew the cause but even then they did not share their feelings. I wish they had expressed. I wish they had understood their feelings I wish they had given a poignant hug to each other and said "They love each other".

Their destiny had something else. They had to meet dead end very soon and they would even not to be able to say FAREWELL to themselves and they would never meet, never ever.....

Everybody was happy except Pushpraj and Jyotsna.... Why didn't they break the silence, stop this hiding? Why didn't they take themselves back to life? They only had to express three true words to each other by breaking the silence..... "I LOVE YOU", someone from both of them should have said and "I Love you too" would have been the response to the one who said but dead end was strongly waiting to wrap them in its arms.....

"The rings were exchanged not the love".

After the engagement, Jyotsna was completely lost. She was like she had lost something important, like she lost her life and does not want to live anymore. She knew she had lost Pushpraj and so lost herself as well.....

That was Pushpraj's last Wednesday with Jyotsna, when she came to the office not for work but to resign from service. Her eyes were wet. Pushpraj was very sure that she had cried a lot and she was still crying as she was in teary eyes. Jyotsna's eyes as if were trying to say that she wanted to be with him, she didn't want to lose him and she can't live without him.

Her eyes were downcast, she was not able to maintain Intense Eye contact with Pushpraj. Her voice was breaking, and he felt her vasps as well. Again they both knew what they want? Why was that happening? But even then they didn't express their feelings on the screen of love. Jyotsna walked in the cabin and kept resignation letter on the table without saying any single word.....

Pushpraj: Hi, How are you?

Jyotsna: I am not good.

Pushpraj: What happened?

Jyotsna: Parents are not keeping well.

Pushpraj: What happened?

Jyotsna: They are unwell and they require personal care and attention.

Pushpraj: What is there in the envelop?

Jyotsna: I can't work here.

Pushpraj: What? I am sorry..... What did you say?

Jyotsna: Please open and read and relieve me from my services.

Pushpraj: But, why do you want to leave?

Jyotsna: I have to, to look after my parents.

Pushpraj: I understand dear Jyotsna. Resignation is not required for this, take leave for 10, 15 days or may be a month but please don't leave like this.

Jyotsna: I am sorry, I can't be here anymore. Bye.

Pushpraj: Jyotsna, listen..... I need you my friend. Please don't leave me like this.

Jyotsna: I am sorry, Take better care.... Bye.....

Jyotsna did not listen; she left immediately and kept her phone off. In life there's always one person that no matter what they have done to you, you just still can't let them go. Pushpraj tried his best to stop her but she didn't listen. She left as if she didn't want to see him anymore. But yes, she had shed tears and left. He knew it was love behind all but still couldn't dare to say her, nor did she.

Pushpraj was sitting and crying badly in his cabin. He too lost everything. He lost his love, his smile, life as these all left away with Jyotsna. He tried to call Jyotsna but her number was switched off..... He was feeling extremely down and sad.....

Khushbu the receptionist was a good friend of Jyotsna. Pushpraj didn't know however Khushbu was very close to Pushpraj as well. Pushpraj didn't know that Jyotsna was sharing everything about their relationship to Khushbu.....

Khushbu saw Pushpraj crying. She saw his teary eyes which she had never seen before. She entered in the cabin and said that she knows the cause behind his disappointment. Pushpraj asked her in harsh tone to move out of the cabin and leave him alone for a while. But she didn't go, she stayed there and said; "Jyotsna loves you". Listening this statement Pushpraj held his head up and asked; "How do you know?" "Are you sure?" Say that you are not lying? Jyotsna had revealed Khushbu that she loved him a lot and so she resigned as she can't see Pushpraj getting married and she cannot bear working together anymore. She said that Jyotsna never expressed only because she did not want to lose a true and the only best friend that she had.

Pushpraj was happy now but demoralized too. He was cursing himself that why didn't he tell Jyotsna about his feelings, emotions? Why didn't he tell that he wanted to have her as a soul mate? Why didn't he tell that he wanted to marry? He was determined now and he committed himself that those which he could not say to Jyotsna before would say it the same day.

He was crying, his tears did not stop rolling out on his face. Because he knew that was a pain, a pain of love which did not stop Vaporizing from his eyes as tears..... He took his bike and went to the bus stop thinking he would find Jyotsna there. However, he could not. He rode his bike for Sudarshanganj and reached there. He reached the bus stop. He didn't go to her house. He called her back again but her number was switched off. He then called on landline and luckily it was her who picked up.

Pushpraj: "I Love You" I want to be with you. Please come and meet me for the last time at the bus stop.

Jyotsna: Hmmm.... ok

She was there in just 05 minutes as if she was waiting for this moment and was in hurry to respond back with three magical words saying "I Love you too".

She was crying and she said.....

Jyotsna: You are mistaken, there are no such feelings and her eyes were down cast.

Pushpraj: I don't know. I only know that I love you, I need you. And I love you more than you do because my heart knows that I am there in your heart. Come on! I can't wait anymore dear Jyotsna, we have been hiding our feelings a lot. Let's express it now and become one..... I Love you dear, say that you love me.

Jyotsna: Hugged him tightly. It was the first hug and it was a poignant hug. She didn't say anything. She was gasping and only crying.

Pushpraj: Jyotsna, you love me right?

Jyotsna: Hmmm..... I love you like anything.....

That day, the love was expressed.....

They love each other, they knew now. But they will never be together, they were unaware.....

10

JYOTSNA BACKED OFF. LOVE FAILED

Jyotsna was not ready and didn't support Pushpraj's decision about breaking the engagement with the girl of Bhimapur. Neither Jyotsna wanted engagement to brake nor she wanted to remain away from him. Finally the same day they discussed and decided to break the engagement and marry later. Both of them were scared as they knew the consequences of the step they planned to take up. They knew they would face unfavorable circumstances which would be unavoidable..... But they were determined and were ready to face all predicaments.

The same day Pushpraj boarded bus in the evening and left for Bhimapur to meet the girl's family and letting them know about dismissal of the engagement.

He reached Pari's house (the girl whom he got engaged) and first he met Pari and said her that he can't marry as he loved Jyotsna. She didn't respond, she just went to the kitchen and maybe she said the same to her mother. Pushpraj was standing outside and then her father shouted his name loudly. Pushpraj after listening his name he came inside. Pari's father asked; "Is this true, that you don't want to marry my daughter?" Pushpraj said, "Yes". He also said he was going to marry someone else.

Pari's elder brother slapped, abused and said hell lot of things. It was like people were taking turns to abuse, clobber, and thrash him. He was clobbered badly in front of Pari by his elder & younger brother. However, it was Pushpraj's mistake that he got engaged to a girl and now wanted to break. He accepted everything as a punishment of his deeds. Her younger brother said he would call police and put him behind the bars. Her father said; he would file FIR against him. Pushpraj said very politely to them that, yes, he was a culprit and he deserved punishment. He also said them to take any action against him which they want only because he was a culprit.

He was bleeding from jaws and he ran away from there saving his life. He came back to Harinagar and explained everything to Jyotsna. She got scared of the consequences that would even be worst coming ahead. She did not ask him about his health. She was not concerned about the pain that his body was suffering through rather she was concerned more about herself that her name should not flash anywhere in the entire scenario. He promised he would never bring any pain to Jyotsna. He promised, she would be kept away from all problems and unfavorable circumstances and he stood tall on his commitments that he made to Jyotsna.

Pushpraj wanted to shift to Roshanabad as he had an opportunity. So he got interviewed in a company and had to join. He wanted Jyotsna as well to join him at Roshanabad. She too was fine with it.

He received a call from Bhimapur police station about the FIR filed against him saying that he demanded for Rs. 10 lakhs and a car. And he broke the engagement only because Pari's family was not able to manage. The charges were wrong because he didn't ask for dowry and he was called to Bhimapur police station.

Pushpraj was stressed but determined to face everything strongly. He shared this with Jyotsna. Jyotsna was scared as she was concerned more about her image. She started negating him, avoiding him as people in the office were also taunting, teasing and blaming him that because of her, Pushpraj broke the engagement.

Pushpraj spoke to a lawyer friend practicing in Harinagar Civil Court and asked him to look after the matter. Pushpraj was taking care of all these but he didn't give any pain to Jyotsna. He was rushing to High Court for stay, for interim bail. Visiting court, standing in the witness box in front of judge which had never ever happened before.

Jyotsna was getting tensed day by day and Pushpraj was consoling her throughout.

11

LOVE TOOK HIS BEATS AWAY

Once a day Pushpraj was in Roshanabad as he went there to organize job for Jyotsna and he had a very positive response from one of an organization. He was very happy as he was thinking that Jyotsna would join him there at Roshanabad next month.

It was 10:00 pm. He was sitting in Volvo bus for Harinagar. He thought of letting Jyotsna know about the good news of her job. He called and said; he had almost got a job for her and most probably she would join next month onwards. The response from Jyotsna's end was very disappointing and demoralizing. She said;

Jyotsna: Pushpraj don't call me again. I don't want to keep any relation with you.

Pushpraj: What happened? Why you are saying so? Please don't say like that?

Jyotsna: I can't carry the blame anymore, everybody is saying, because of me you broke the engagement. I can't tolerate now.

Pushpraj: Jyotsna, please don't bother about others. It's our life. I will manage. Trust me. Avoid people's saying.

Jyotsna: Please forgive me & don't ever dare to call.

Pushpraj: Jyotsna, I will die, please don't say like this.....

Jyotsna: (disconnected).

The bus reached at a Dhaba in Hameerganj. He thought of having dinner as he was hungry. He took first bite but couldn't swallow because paralysis had hit on his mouth and his mouth moved and got displaced towards left. He was neither able to swallow nor drink. He was not able to speak even. He got much tensed. He felt as if he was going to die. He was holding his mouth and trying to place that back to its position so that he speaks clearly. But this was paralysis hit and flicks which was trying to overpower the whole nervous system of the body and make him living dead.

He immediately went back to his seat and dialed Jyotsna's number to speak to her;

Jyotsna: Please don't disturb. I am already tensed.

Pushpraj: (Holding mouth and trying to speak but stammering, gasping) I don't know, what's happening? It seems I am dying. Please say you love me. Say that you love me. Don't marry me until I get things fixed. But say that you love me. My nerves, the entire body is losing control. It's going senseless. My friend, I will die. Please say that you love me (He was crying badly).

Jyotsna: Please take care of yourself and bother me never.

Pushpraj: Jyotsna, I am dying. For god's sake say that you love me please, just say for once.

Jyotsna: I hate you?? If you dare to call me again I too will file FIR against you.

Pushpraj had nervous breakdown behind his left ear which started giving unbearable pain to him. He was groaning badly. And then his left leg had hamstring in the calves muscle. He was not able to move his leg and then gradually his left leg got numb and then the left hand. Thereafter right leg, right hand and then entire body were paralyzed. He became a living dead. He died that day in love as he lost his soul mate. And to live without her was unacceptable for him. His entire body was paralyzed and that is why he was not able to sense anything, not able to move. He was only able to understand and sense the feelings.

The bus reached Harinagar at around 03:45 AM. Everybody got down from the bus but he couldn't. The conductor saw Pushpraj in pathetic condition thought he was a drunkard and heavily drunk. Abusing Pushpraj, the conductor and driver took him up and left him at the bus stop with his shoulder bag.

Pushpraj was left at bus stop and was there as living dead for almost 10:00 hours. His phone was switched off. His parents were trying his number but could not connect. They knew about his visit to Harinagar and then coming back to home. He would have urinated 5-6 times. He would have done pee plumbing many times. His whole body was covered by flies all over. He had never dreamt of being in such condition. It's better to die rather being in such condition. He and his heart were still expecting Jyotsna to turn back in life. But it was the end as the chapter of Jyotsna had ended that day when he was armed by paralysis. The flies were entering his mouth, his nose, ears, sitting on eyes but he was not able fly those flies away. He died every moment that day. His heart was crying for Jyotsna. It was his true love for Jyotsna.

His parents reached to the bus stop after searching him at various possible places where he could be. But they found him at the bus stop. His mother took him in arms and cried loudly like anything. She held him as if Pushpraj was no more and Pushpraj was feeling sorry about himself that because of him, his mother was shedding tears. Pushpraj's mother was asking him what had happened. But he was not able to utter even a single word clearly. His mother was crying, groaning so badly that her breath was falling short. Pushpraj was also crying but tears could not come out, his heart was crying badly internally. He couldn't see his mother and father crying badly as like never before.

He was taken to a hospital where doctor gave up after a day saying he should be taken to Roshanabad.

He was admitted in a hospital at Roshanabad for 49 days where he was advised for bed rest for 06 months. Jyotsna never called him after that. Pushpraj was a soft skills trainer and singer who wanted to establish himself as a singer in Bollywood Industry. He had owned 02 medals and 18 awards in singing. He was very much concerned about his voice. He was praying to God and wishing that let his voice be alright and rest not required. Because it was his voice by which he was singing and delivering training. While sleeping, inside the blanket, he used to murmur "Good morning Boys & Girls, Hi, this is Pushpraj". He used to say this by holding his mouth which had got displaced towards left. People used to laugh on him, thinking he was gone mad. But he didn't bother. He just had one aim to rise back again.

On 49th day, he came to know about an interview. He wanted to appear for the interview but it was in Bhimapur. He decided to appear and to go to Bhimapur. The interview was on the next day. His right part of the body had started functioning now. The left had problem especially in left hand, left edge of the mouth and eye. Whenever Pushpraj would speak he would sense the paralysis flicks on mouth and eyes especially when he was tensed.

The 50th day he decided to move to Bhimapur for the interview because he had her sister's marriage in few months. And he had promised to her sweet sister to gift her long car. And that was only possible if he took up a job. Pushpraj was unwell and he could not walk without walker. He got up from the bed. His father asked; where was he moving? He replied he was going to washroom. His father asked, shall he come along? He replied; No! He would manage. Pushpraj didn't go to the washroom. He came to bus stop. There he had French cut shave as his beard had grown longer and then purchased goggle to let interviewer not sense his physical illness.

Before boarding bus for Bhimapur, he called his father to inform him about his movement for interview. He reached Bhimapur where he got interviewed and bagged a job.

His dream of gifting his sister her long Car got true. He gifted her car of Rs. 8.73 lakh on her wedding. However the car was on finance but even then it always made him feel good that he made his dream come true.

Pushpraj was back to life. He never blamed Jyotsna for those circumstances. He thought that maybe it was her compulsion to do so..... Pushpraj loved Jyotsna. He couldn't have Jyotsna in his life. But he gave his best shot.

12

"GURPREET"-HIS LOVE, HIS ONLY DESIRE AND HIS LAST WISH (LOVE HITS BACK)

"Somebody likes his song,
Somebody likes his thought,
Somebody wants to be always remembered,
Somebody wants to see him on the top.
Somebody wants him to write for her till death.
Somebody calls him Bhoot,
Somebody is called Gauri by him
And that somebody is GURPREET".

They started as strangers, left as friends but Pushpraj wanted to meet back again neither as stranger nor as friend but as soul mates forever.

Who is GURPREET?

GURPREET is Love, A love that breeds within

She is life, without her it has no meaning....

She is the most beautiful girl with fair conducts he has ever seen in his life. GURPREET is his WAIT OF AGES.....

Love attacked Pushpraj after 6.5 years. He met her many times but didn't realize he was being armed by love. He realized when he saw a dream and it was all about his and her heart. Their hearts were crying. He saw her in his heart and himself in hers. The both hearts were crying as they were no more theirs. The hearts were crying in pain as they were sensing threat of being separated and going away from each other.

Pushpraj immediately got up and his dream broke. And wrote an article titled as: Do I need to worry?" It was the day, when he was hit by love after so long..... And thereafter he gave that girl a name i.e. "GURPREET".

Do I need to worry?

Do I need to worry? "But for whom? And for what?

- "Do I need to worry for the one whom I don't know.

What am I worried about? "Shall I tell you the fact?".... I know the answer of the cause behind my sadness but I don't want my heart and soul to plant the fact in my heart and soul.

Dear Heart, let me be in dilemma for a while, let me cherish those moments. That spent with her, No matter.... I am no one to her but want to be hers....

Am I worrying about her? Or else worried about losing her & knowing the fact "SHE CAN'T MINE".... And the chapter finishes.

"No".... It's life, it's not a chapter of any book.... It's the love breeding in my heart and soul from "Sooooo Long" for HER. How Am I supposed to live without her? This question still has no answer.... I have started loving her as if I love her from so long.... It's something, she needs to understand and sense deep inside her heart.... Please, Dear Heart, "Ask her to peep inside her heart and soul as the answer lies within".....

So, I am worried for everything.... I want to live life, I want to live at its fullest. I want to smile, cry But with you "GURPREET".

Yes, I am worrying and I will worry until she is mine or else. I depart silently having left everything behind and close my own chapter......**"WAITING FOR YOU ALWAYS"**

He sent the write up to GURPREET that he wrote..... He was very sure, she was also slightly hit by love and her heart was armed in love arms of Pushpraj. They had just met, maybe it was 7-8 days old relationship when love found place to breed within their hearts & souls.

GURPREET was always seen sad, down, unhappy whenever he would meet her. She used to draw abstract images in her notebook, on chair's writing pad. She used to draw hearts even and write something and then erase. Her sadness was very painful, unbearable to Pushpraj. He too was sensing sadness seeing her sad. He was much tensed, sad, seeing her sad whenever they met. It was love. It's very obvious, when she smiled, he smiled as if he got treasure. When she cried, he cried as if he had lost something i.e. important. When she laughed, he laughed as if he had never laughed before when she hugged, he found peace of eternity and then he lived for her, he died for her. He did everything to bring smile on her face. And that was love.....

Her sadness was becoming intolerable and unbearable. He was pining and he decided to ask her the cause behind her gloomy face which was driving him sad like anything.

He asked her about her sadness and then got shocked. She was suffering from "Migraine" from last 05 years. And she said that she experienced it daily. She was getting pain on both sides of her head that

Felt throbbing or pulsing. She stroke her head on the walls when her headache went unbearable. She also

said; that it was difficult to predict when a migraine attack was going to happen. And she would go mad and felt like killing herself. The worst thing was when she said she was not afraid of DEATH. She was not under any medical diagnosis for migraine and this put Pushpraj under trauma. He said to GURPREET. Please don't talk about death. You don't know there are people who would need you. This was the first statement of his that he expressed indirectly to her that "It was him who needed GURPREET".

Pushpraj was very down and he started bothering GURPREET and she started occupying a huge space in his heart and her conducts were breeding within his heart and soul. His behavior was bothering her so much and bothered her like anything throughout life.

He bothered her like "He had been waiting for her, waiting for so long".

He wanted to know what GURPREET bothered so much that affected her mental peace and ruined her health. He asked a day on what's app. That day his love for GURPREET grew stronger than ever and he took a firm determination to have her in his life by any means.

You know what, those who are dear to you, the ones whom you love, you will never stop bothering and taking pain for them because the absence of pain is death. So when something no longer bothers you, you have died to that thing. And he bothered and took pain for GURPREET a lot.

GURPREET was not at all hesitant to reveal the cause behind her sufferings. She was going to share which she had never shared before to anyone. She emphasized and said it was only him whom she shared everything and nobody else. "This was a matter of Trust". Don't know how but she trusted him and that's why she shared everything to him.

Pushpraj asked her "Did she trust him? "She said "No". He wanted to know, then why was she sharing her personals, if she didn't trust? She said; because Pushpraj was a stranger and put very far away from her area. But even then he asked "if she didn't trust, then how could see share?" She was ambiguous, maybe she didn't want to bring fact on her mouth that she trusted him like no one else and that is why she shared him which she had never shared to anybody?

This "stranger Pushpraj" was no more a stranger now for her. They both knew who they are? They knew they are more than friends....

She tried killing her by all possible ways. 04 times she cut her nerves. She was lost when love entered in her life. She was betrayed in love. She felt broken and alone. Depression and anxiety were draining her physically and emotionally. She lost her true self. She started smoking, drinking alcohol and she got a bad company where she ruined herself. Yes, she tried all possible ways to end her life for someone who didn't even care for her.... This all happened to her when she was in 11th Standard, i.e. five years ago. She wanted to join NIFT but she couldn't only because she died in love for love which was one sided and that too it was from her end. She was exploited badly. She loved and she made true love but she was being

Used every single moment and betrayed. She lost everything. She is now left up with pain, sorrows which are pining her towards death.

After these circumstances she kept herself disconnected from everybody. In fact, she did not share anything to her parents. She was very silent. She was not talking to anybody. She was not herself?

Pushpraj said to GURPREET after having chat. He said to her that he is feeling very special and lucky that she shared having count on him. He also said to her that he doesn't trust himself, so she should never share such personal things to any one not even him except parents. He said "Nobody can be as loyal as your parents". Because they always love, care and bother. And their love is always unconditional. He asked her to promise him that she would never share it to anybody except parents. She said, yes she would never ever. He said that her parents will always keep her image positive, will never defame and they are the only true and genuine friends. Pushpraj asked her to change her what's app status to "BACK TO LIFE". And she did it.

He was in love and now he started bothering her like his soul mate. His nights were going restless. He wanted to meet her and counsel her for all and make her feel that "she is not just special, but important to her parents".

Pushpraj prepared a PPT presentation with sad Piano instrumental in background. So he asked her to show him her parent's photo and her childhood photo. The objective was to use all those pictures in presentation to make her realize that she is not alone. She is not lost.

Pushpraj started working on presentation to give his best shot to her for her better life. He took 8-10 days. Finally he was ready and asked her to meet him for the same. He got projector, laptop and speakers set. She came and don't know, why HIS eyes were teary, as if he would cry in front of her. He was going very emotional that day as he knew about the tragedy and the illness she was going through. He wanted to say her right there that "he loved her".

She was smiling and "he" was like breathing her smile in his heart and soul which was filling life which he had lost long years ago. Her smile was heart catching which would sprinkle fair love all over in his heart. But he could sense deep pain behind her smile.

He showed her a presentation and mentioned below is what he showed:

It's a Girl!

Hurrah! The girl is born. Let the name be GURPREET.....

SHE IS MORE precious than jewels.

Daddy's girl and Mommy's world

College life.

Love enters the life

Gets betrayed in love

More broken then one think

Broken, Alone

Depression and Anxiety were draining her physically and emotionally. She lost her true self.

She tried all possible ways to end her life for someone who didn't even care for her.

Rays of hope enters her life and tries to make her understand that you are more than just a break up.

Even if you have gone too far....

Remember your parents are always there to hold your hand.

Now comes up.....

GURPREET's few happiest moments

Naughty..... A bit kiddish.... Funny and lot more....

A bit kiddish.... Enjoying life at fullest

A girl who targeted for NIFT.....

Photo shoots with brother.... Was beaten by mummy for this epic shot.

Cute and sweet sister of her brother! But does not find herself a sweet sister anymore!

The best shot again....?? GURPREET, looking a bit notorious.... Free from tension, stress.

Happy GURPREET and Real GURPREET.... But is lost now......

Mummy's love for you GURPREET....!.....!

It's time to love her Back.....

The most wonderful gift ever..... Your MOM & DAD..... Your God and true FRIEND.....!!

They would feel sad....?? You are sad..... Time to make them feel proud.....!......!...... Rise up and suit yourself for success.....

I still think you're BEAUTIFUL. Trust one, I still think.... You are beautiful by your heart soul..... Don't curse yourself..... You did no wrong.... I know my heart knows..... Never ever do this......

Please never ever feel down..... I sense the sorrow everyday.... Kick off your past...... please MOVE ON..... Want you to SUCCEEED.....

Enough with the past..... Time to live in present and secure the FUTURE BRITHER..... Be Happy always!....!....!.....! Keep smiling!....!....!.....! You have a sweet smile!....!....!.....!

You ARE BEAUTIFUL by your HEART & SOUL.... You DID NO WRONG..... YOU GET THAT..... YOU DO.... NO WRONG.... TRUST ME.....

Looking forward to see you in MNC....!....!....!.....!

If you need your parents, JUST CALL THEM. IF THEY ARE FOR YOU, NO MATTER HOW BIG OR SMALL YOUR PROBLEM IS

Your relationship ended not your life...... It's time to move on it's time to return back to life....

She cried without tear. She realized she is someone even she realized she is someone to somebody. She realized that she is somewhere in somebody's heart. Her heart cried that day a lot. Pushpraj sensed her feelings. He was not able to speak after that. He had no words because his heart was shedding tears and wanted to tell her that "she was his world". She meant everything. Pushpraj no longer existed without GURPREET. He cried because he wanted GURPREET to be his, "forever and ever"......

GURPREET's trust now even grew deeper and stronger for him. She knew, she can count on him.

Pushpraj's intention was not just to achieve her. But he truly from core of his heart wanted GURPREET to be happy, healthy and successful. He wanted her to grow, progress, touch the zenith, go higher and higher where no tensions, depressions reach to her and she was surrounded by success and happiness only. "He loved her, was that a mistake? He bothered her, was that a sin? He desired her in his life, was that a crime?". Is love punishment" Is love hell? Whatever it was, one thing was inevitable, and nobody could stop him from loving GURPREET, Nobody in this world.

Once a day he asked GURPREET to come in suit (Ethic wear). She didn't negate and the next day she was in creamish white suit with light green tippet hung on left shoulder. She looked truly beautiful. She was like Sikkhni (Punjabi girl in ethnic wear). She never minded. She was always in suit whenever he asked. She started following his each and everything and so did Pushpraj.

She wanted him to record songs and sent it to her. The first song that she asked her was from the movie "Airlift" (Bollywood movie) and the track was "Tanu itna mai pyaar kara". He got it recorded and sent it to her. She was happy enough to listen the song in his voice. And then she desired him to send his songs every day. And he too committed. She said that she loved his voice, his songs, and his articles.

He started writing songs, articles only for her. He wrote madly for her. It's insane that how can somebody get so drowned in love. It was just 3.5 months only and he would have met her 15-20 times. Talking about hours, he would have not spent more than 30 hours in those 15-20 meets.... Then how did he go so deep in her love? He now remembered nothing. He only remembered to write and to write for GURPREET as "She wanted him to write always throughout life till death.... But will she be there to read his articles, to listen his songs always throughout life till death???? Whenever he thought about this question he died that moment, his breath left soul, his life left hope and he pined away..... But one thing he would never stop is writing about GURPREET, whatever the condition was. Whether he was dying, pining, crying anything but he would never stop writing because GURPREET would wait for his write-ups. He knew there would be a time when GURPREET will never have reach to his articles, songs even then he would write only because he had committed. He would remain loyal to his commitment forever till death and he wanted this somebody "who was GURPREET" to be remembered always till the end of universe in his write-ups".

A time came when Pushpraj had to depart to Lamjung. And he wanted to meet GURPREET for the last time and spare time with her but it was impossible, she had to go out of the city by 08:10 AM the very same day. However, she called; she said; she wanted to meet Pushpraj and say good bye. Her hair was wet and opened. She came in suit carrying 05 greeting cards. She gave that to him and said Good Bye....

And Pushpraj was like his soul was leaving his body and meeting death. He had purchased a chocolate pack and few candies for her. He gave that to her. She departed.... And that was the saddest moment which was unbearable. He was lost when she departed. He stood there, seeing at her and after a minute she was out of vision but he stood there for 30 minutes expecting he would get a last glimpse of this somebody girl his love, his GURPREET.

Those 05 cards made by her. He couldn't dare to open those cards and read. He just saw 05 cards having hearts all over, beautifully designed and prepared by GURPREET for him. He was never gifted so many cards that too by one. Yes, this was love that he considered and sensed or maybe he misunderstood. Don't know but he strongly believed that it was GURPREET's love for him, love that of a soul mate for a soul mate.

He was travelling for Lamjung by train. He was feeling restless. He didn't know what to do what not" He opened the cards and read them with curious eyes, feeling pain of separation at every single word. His tears didn't stop the whole journey to Lamjung. He had hand towel covered his eyes to soak the tears rolling out in pain of love. He then wrote his pain on paper.....

"I am crying, I cried a lot reading those 05 cards, seeing all the images pasted and drawn and the infinite incised hearts pasted which are actually beating but in pain. You are asking me to smile and read your heartiest thoughts of the cards. Dear GURPREET, I opened and forcefully brought smile on my face which I am sure looked weird to the co-passengers in train as this is not my smile, the real smile. I tried to wear smile but later, reading lines one after another, your lines fetched tears in my eyes and I shed ocean of tears and I am still crying. It's not just tears, it's the desire of heart and soul never leaving and keeping you away. My heart is not that big but it has a place where you can live in under shower of love, fragrance of happiness, ocean of feelings & true emotions, essence of trust and respect which are only for you and it's limited only for you.

Dear GURPREET, you lie a lot.....Here is a small poem for you....

"BURY ME SO I LIVE

THE BREATH IS ON HOLD

FUNERALIZE ME SO I LIVE

THE WAIT FOR YOU IS ON HOLD

LET ME GO AS I CAN'T LET YOU GO

SO THE CHAPTER OF LOVE REMAINS UNTOLD

FINISH THE LOVE & LIFE CHAPTER

SO THE DEATH ARMS ME & HOLD

BURY ME......

He made GURPREET listen that write up and poem and said her to stay connected forever and ever..... She promised, she would be....

Pushpraj was in hospital the next day when he reached Lamjung. His breath fell short. He was suffering from breathing problem which had never happened before to him. It was like his breathes wanted GURPREET's presence there. He was all alone there. There was nobody to help him out except the hospital staff. He was on the bed and was dripped oxygen and his heart was praying to lord that he wants to live, he doesn't want to die, why does Lord put him in such deadly conditions whenever he

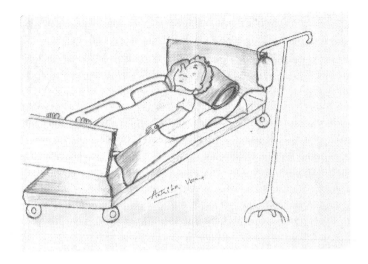

Made true and genuine love? What did he want? He was telling to Lord that he just bothered GURPREET and was scared of losing her. Can Lord help him? Can he bring GURPREET in his life? He kept waiting for Lord's response. But he knew, he would have GURPREET in his life a day.....

His phone was switched off. GURPREET called him 69 times. It was the first time when she called him so many times. The 70th call was answered by him. Her voice on phone was like gasping. She was tensed as it was more than 24 hours when they didn't speak to each other. Seeing her concern, pushpraj again fell in love. When he told her about his sickness she was extremely tensed and bothered for him.

He was in a University at Lamjung and near to the square there was a cafe. The café had a studio where anyone could perform anything related to music. He was there for 05 days. He visited the café the 03rd day as first two days he was unwell. He went all the three days and performed his own composed song for GURPREET there at the café. First two days he couldn't put GURPREET on phone to make her listen. But the third day he wanted his composition to be listened and he wanted her to listen. He said to GURPREET that he was going to make GURPREET listen her live. So she asked Pushpraj to call her at 09:00 pm as she would be done with her dinner.

He reached the café and dialed her no, put her online. He kept the lyrics on the stand, held Microphone in left and mobile phone in right. "Tujhe Khona Ye Sochna Nahi" was his self-composed track that he had sung for her. But GURPREET said the voice was not clear. He decided to sing again as he composed and performed it for GURPREET. It didn't make sense as it was not clear to her. He re-performed holding microphone in left and requested a spectator to hold the phone standing near to the speaker to give her a clarity and better feel of the song. This time it was nice. She said it was better and clear. You know what, she was very excited about his song. And Pushpraj wished, he could have her live there.

GURPREET always requested to Pushpraj, that he should find a suitable girl for himself and marry. She knew that Pushpraj was married and his relationship was complicated as he got separated from his wife right after the next day of their marriage. Pushpraj always said that he had imagined a girl named GAURI in his imagination from last 6.5 years. He had always said; the day he would find somebody like Gauri, he would propose and keep a marriage proposal. Pushpraj said her about Gauri after few days of their meeting and especially when GURPREET a day said on chat that she can marry anybody who remains loyal to her and lives for her. She said; she would dedicate herself to him. She loves being in joint family. She too said she would be loyal and stay responsible for her duties as daughter-in-law for everybody. Pushpraj was very happy after having such noble thoughts because he never got love. He always wished to have a wife who would love him and his family. He wished, that before a wife she must be a good daughter-in-law which did not happen. That's why they were separated.

When GURPREET shared her thoughts, pushpraj was very happy as he wished to have like GURPREET in life by any means. He wanted to have her because she had turned him sincere, serious about his future and career. She was the only girl who was an inspirational source to him. The result was that; he became singer. He gained passion only when GURPREET entered in life. He wanted to be a singer and he was lost. Now his wish of being singer had taken life and the result was that he wrote many songs though all written for GURPREET in just 2.5 months. She said she liked his articles as well and he wrote many articles for GURPREET. He wrote for GURPREET and nobody else because she wanted him to write forever till death. Pushpraj was no more like he was before. He was a star which lost its existence but now he was rising, emerging, getting back to life and became a shining star due to GURPREET's faith on him. That's why he loved him a lot and wanted her to be there in his life as soul mate till eternity. Is it a crime that he loved? Is it a sin, if somebody waited for true love? Doesn't love strike back in life?

He desired GURPREET and she was his final wish. He always told her about Gauri that he wanted to have a girl who is ditto Gauri. He also said that after a year he was going to find her. She was eager to know about Gauri. She didn't know that she herself was Gauri. Pushpraj said she would be the first one whom he would tell about Gauri but after a year. But GURPREET wanted to know at that instance itself. He didn't tell and her eagerness grew like anything. She knew that he was going to take her name. May be she was curious to know and to listen her own name.... She kept asking but he didn't tell. He kept saying that GURPREET was like Gauri. She had all the attributes of Gauri. This is what he always said her. He also said that only Gurpreet was like Gauri.

He didn't actually know whether she was in love or not but he felt a sort of tender curiosity. Somewhere, yes, she loved him.

"YOU ARE Gauri": Pushpraj revealed to GURPREET on phone chat. She was shocked. He said to her "Be with me throughout life.... YOU ARE Gauri". He asked her "Can she spend her life with him"? "Can she be Gauri to him?" She said she does not know. She cannot rely on future. She was afraid of future results. She said her family will never accept. She said she does not want to take any pain now. She doesn't want to spoil herself. She said because of Pushpraj, she has gained confidence to live and to grow in life. Because of him she feels, she exists and her existence is worth. She fears that she might have the worst case scenarios back again if she again falls in love, if she is betrayed. She fears that she will be no more if she ever comes across such circumstances. She said that she is very lucky to know that Pushpraj loves him and has true love for her. She would be happy to be with him. But she was confused. She said she didn't know.

Pushpraj became sad after having GURPREET's response. But she was right. Being a girl it was difficult to break the chain and boundaries. He asked, how about if her parents allow her to stay with Pushpraj? He meant having marriage and then staying by saying so. She said she would go with anyone who is recommended by her parents. And then she said a statement which disappointed Pushpraj a lot? "I don't have that kind of feelings for you". GURPREET said to Pushpraj. Pushpraj shattered and paused the chat for 22 minutes.

Pushpraj felt that he should have never said that GURPREET was Gauri. He was confused what he should do then? He lost Jyotsna 6.5 years ago, lost his image only because he didn't express his feelings to Jyotsna at the right time. He almost lost GURPREET because he proposed. May be he did that very early. He discontinued chat and started keeping distance from GURPREET. He literally wanted to put everything to an end except writing for her which she wrote in cards and expressed desire. He disconnected her.....

She wrote a long mail. Gave 100 + calls. Calling day & night. Calls coming at 01:00 A.M., 02:00 A.M. as if she didn't sleep that day. He read his mail where she said "love and trust is a gradual process. May be someday love happens to her and things go fine. What kind of love is this that you disconnected? Those who love they never stay disconnected because they can never be away from their beloved", she wrote in mail and messages. It means she was also in love. 100 + calls day and night, mails, messages shows what, her restlessness towards Pushpraj, Isn't that love? Isn't she is love? She is just not able to dare and say.

The longest, deadliest and sweetest conversation.

Just listen to me first. How can you judge me like this? Hey! You, listen, listen to me first (GURPREET spoke very harshly to Pushpraj):

Pushpraj; GURPREET, you are speaking as if you are speaking to a goon, a rowdy. Dear GURPREET, no girl has ever spoken to me like this before. I didn't expect such harsh tone from the one whom I admire the most (He cried and was gasping).

This scene happened as GURPREET promised to send him 02 songs in her own voice almost 20-25 days ago. She always had a cause behind not sending to him. He asked her to record and send a song in her voice. And Pushpraj said that "she didn't want to send him that's why she made lame excuses every day when he asked for the same. And her response was very harsh, that was truly unexpected and heart breaking.

Pushpraj blocked her contact number. After 24 hours When he unblocked her contact no, he found 233 calls from her, messages and a long mail asking sorry.

That day she called Pushpraj from an unknown number and she said please don't disconnect "Apko kasam hai meri (By Me). He didn't listen and cut the call.

Later, Pushpraj texted her; I want to speak to you for the last time", he texted to GURPREET.

That was the longest and the sweetest telephonic conversation they ever had. They spoke for 04 hours and 47 minutes till 05:25 AM. And that was the last.

After talking over phone he again sensed love because she was curious to talk to him but pushpraj wasn't. But later he felt positive and realized that yes love is a gradual process and it would gradually happen.

She genuinely felt sorry that day.....

THE DARKEST DAY & EVERYTHING FINISHED.

Pushpraj was like out of his mind. Yes, it was a blunder that he did. It was his mistake and everything finished.

He felt as if he was hurting her because she always said "He can never understand her". So he deleted her contact number and blocked. His intention was neither to ignore nor hurt. He just wanted her to stay away from tensions which would always put her in stress due to his conducts. She said that "Pushpraj has lost his value and importance. He was not the one whom she had met". So he disconnected her for her happiness not to hurt. After knowing that she was blocked, she dropped Pushpraj a message "why is he ignoring?" He called her and said that he did not want to hurt. He said He is more than a friend and so he bothered her. She asked what you mean "more than a friend?" You are just a friend-GURPREET said. In response, pushpraj said "he is not a friend" then she asked "who is he?" He felt broken like anything when he was asked "who is he?" The girl who trusted him blindly like anything asked "who is he"? Listening this pushpraj disconnected and then called her back after a while saying that "He was no one and He is No one" to her and then disconnected.

Pushpraj called her on her mobile no and she said "SORRY WRONG NO". He felt like heart attack. He called again and she said "You are dialing a wrong no. please don't call". He called again and this time the phone was switched off. He gave 789 calls till morning 06:00 AM, 96 messages but nothing reached to her, neither call nor message. She had broken her SIM CARD and threw away. Pushpraj was shivering. He was suffering from shortness of breath and was sweating. He felt like jumping in front of train and dying but he didn't do because he has many who love him a lot. And he had also promised that he would keep writing for her till death so how could he die? He was sensing abnormal heart rhythms which were going serious and even deadly. He died that day. He truly died. He was disconnected and he was partially disconnected.

Pushpraj missed her badly. He knew that he did mistake. He blocked her many times and now GURPREET did but almost forever. They were connected but they rarely chat and spoke. EVERYTHING CHANGED. But one thing did not "He kept writing for her every day and sent her his entire write up on her mail.....

A Confession to GURPREET (He wrote to confess his mistake)
YOU DID NO WRONG, MY MISTAKE.

YES, it's my mistake or I say your kindness which tolerated my partial emotions called LOVE and put you under the shed of SUFFERINGS.

My mistake, I saw JYOTSNA within you and considered you the same throughout or I say your soft magnanimous heart which sore an unknown character out within for my happiness.

My mistake I wrote articles, songs which my heart forced to do which I never did before or I say your care for my career which bothered and displayed curiosity.

My mistake, I said I want you throughout my life, want you be with me forever and ever or I say your amicable nature which expressed agreement to stay connected whole life.

My mistake, I said you are not just special you are important to me or I say your generosity which didn't carry attitude but remained simple and humble as you are.

My mistake, I said you are inspirational source for the articles, songs, a book transforming me author or I say your sincerity which didn't take any credit rather appreciated my write-ups.

My mistake, I said you are melodious as your act dissolved the melody of love and life within or I say your sweetness which brought me closer to yo9ur melody.

My biggest mistake, I said you are FAKE, I said your conducts are act of formalities, I said you are No one or I say your forgiveness which forgot everything and has kept a partial touch base. A touch base fenced by the thorns of distance which was never before. You have forgotten your harsh words but have not forgiven. I have lost image, value and TRUST.

My mistake, my mistake, my mistake, and hell lot of mistakes I have done. Who is perfect in this world? Who didn't ever commit mistake? Who is not fallible? I knew hurting your soul is a sin and I should be brought under sentence panel for punishment. I will truly repent, I will do everything which would get my image, value back to your life. About trust I never know, will it ever be planted in your heart & soul.

Order me a death punishment. Your ignorance is unbearable I would sense pleasure and joy to offer myself in the arms of death. But remember, a culprit before his death is asked for his last wish. Before departing away, I would want you to ask me my wish and if you ask.... It would be" Am I Pushpraj or No one?"

"HANG ME FOR LOVE, NOOSE ME FOR MY MISTAKE

YOU DID NO WRONG, IT'S MY ENTIRE MISTAKE".

ONLY YOU GURPREET

In cards she wrote that May pushpraj gets all that he wants. But Pushpraj wants only her.

She wrote may his all dreams come true.... But He has only one dream and a goal to have her in reality.

She wrote "Hum hai is pal yahaan jane ho kal kaha, hum mile na mile, rahengi yaadein yaha" but he says he does not want to live in memories. He wants to live with Real GURPREET.

She wrote "Mai rahoon ya na rahoo, tu mujhme kahi baaki rahna and wrote Don't forget me....But he says, he loved you, He loves you. And will love you till death....

He will never stop writing for GURPREET. He is a true lover and he knows She too is a "FAIR LOVER".........

INTEZAAR HAI MUJHE (A desire)

INTEZAAR HAI MUJHE, KE WO MERA
INTEZAAR KARE.... BEGAIRAT NAHI, JO USE
TADPAOON...
WO HOGI MERI, WO BAS MERA AITBAAR
KARE....
CHAHU USE BEPANAAH, INTEZAAR HAI KI WO
BHI CHAHAT KARE...
YE KOI KHILAFAT TO NAHI, JO USE CHAHA....
HU FANAA HONE KO TAIYAAR, BAS WO
IZHAAR KARE....
MERE ISHQ KE SHABAB KO, WO DUA SALAAM
KARE....
MAI KOI DUSHMAN NAHI, JO ISHQ KO GHULAM
KARE.....
HU MAI TO HUMSAFAR-E-ISHQ, JO USKE ISHQ
KE AITRAAM KARE...
KHWAHISH YE BHI HAI, KI IK BAAR WO NAAM
PUKAR KARE....
WO BERAHAM TO NAHI, JO MUJHE TADPAYE....
PUKAARE IS KADAR, KE USKA DIL MERE DIL
SE BAAT KARE....
AAZMAYE WO MERI MOHABBAT, JO SIRF USE
PYAAR KARE....
DIL KOI KHILONA TO NAHI, JO DIYA MAINE....
YE DIL HAI DIL, AUR YE DIL SIRF USE PYAAR
KARE.....
BAS EK KHWAHISH, KI WO KHUDME MUJHE
SHAAMID KARE....

INTEZAAR KHATAM HO AUR HUM ISHQ SARE
AAM KARE....
INTEZAAR HAI MUJHE, KI WO MERA
INTEZAAR KARE.....

Pushpraj (waiting for GURPREET, nothing without
GURPREET).

"SHE WAS THE FAIREST GIRL WITH FAIR
HEART, HE HAD EVER SEEN IN HIS LIFE AND
SO HE DESIRED TO HAVE GURPREET.

Like you or YOU??

"I desire to have someone like YOU. I wish I had met YOU before".... I wish.....I wished..... And still I wish to have someone like YOU in life.....☺☺

Truth lies within heart & soul but takes time to express in words.....

"And sometimes you NEVER express". "YOU BURY YOUR FEELINGS IN THE GRAVEYARD OF YOUR SOUL AND THE LOVE IS FUNERALIZED". You feel like FINISHED. But the heart always awaits for HER as the heart beats pace up the count and express desire to have her anyhow, by any means in life to give LIFE A MEANING.

People say true love never succeeds. It always meets a "DEAD END". Is it true??? May be.... I ummmm.... Actually..... I am not sure.... I don't know...... "I am different". Juliet-Ceaser, Laila-Majnu, Heer-Ranjha-The epic lovers who couldn't meet and never had a happy ending☹☹. Will the same happen to me??? Am I stressed? I think I am bothered about my destiny..

I will not give any second thought thinking about the destiny and future results. As if now, I am positive and sanguine approach towards getting her within. Do you know, who she is?? Do you know, what does she mean to me????

"SHE IS LOVE
A LOVE THAT BREEDS WITHIN
SHE IS LIFE
WITHOUT HER IT HAS NO MEANING"

I want to express and project my feelings on the screen of "LOVE". But I cannot, I fail to reveal the truth to you as I find myself "NO WHERE" in front of "YOU". I feel I have no identity. I want to form an identity to which the entire world gets acquainted with. So that I reach "SOME WHERE" from "NO WHERE". Till than I will conceal the fact within. Once I form a global identity, I am sure.......I would gain confidence to express the feelings breeding in my heart and soul from soooo loooong.

And this time....

"THE HEART SHOULD NOT BE IN DILEMMA, NEITHER THE WORDS SHOULD FUMBLE, NOR SHOULD I FROWN TO SAY".....

"NOT LIKE YOU- I WISH YOU" forever and ever.....

It's not the end.....

What if I am rejected? What if I came to know, I was never in her thoughts, I was never in her heart & soul.... I mean I was "NO ONE AND NO WHERE" to HER.... ☹☹

Will I Arm myself in the arms of DEATH??? Will I chose DEAD END?

No, I will live, I will cherish the moments spent with or without her, thinking about her....

I know it's difficult, very difficult to even imagine LIFE without her. But Death is not the end as the feelings within soul is always ALIVE which remain IMMORTAL and never dies... & the HEART WILL REPEATEDLY WISH THE SAME, WHENEVER IS REBORN AND EXPRESS ITS INCORRIGIBLE DESIRE-

"NOT LIKE YOU-WANT ONLY YOU" Will wait till eternity......

Pushpraj loves Gurpreet and he is waiting for her to be his SOULMATE. He is determined, he will not give up. He can't afford to lose Gurpreet.

"PUSHPRAJ & GURPREET WILL DEFINITELY MEET"

SATISH B3 ANAND

Printed in the United States
By Bookmasters